UNBOTTLING THE Wind

IKE MORAH

authorHOUSE®

AuthorHouse™
1663 Liberty Drive
Bloomington, IN 47403
www.authorhouse.com
Phone: 1-800-839-8640

Published by AuthorHouse   11/07/2012

ISBN: 978-1-4772-8902-0 (sc)
ISBN: 978-1-4772-8901-3 (e)

Library of Congress Control Number: 2012921140

Mr. and Mrs. J. J. Cash were now back home and settling into their new matrimonial home. They had successfully tied the knot, or as Joy would prefer to put it, "they had just gotten hitched." They were now enjoying that bliss of wedlock. This new state of conjugal bliss was new to each of them, but all the same they were enjoying it. She had reminded him that she was now in a state of wifehood and he in a state of husband-hood, if one could put it that way. That was however the only way that she could put their situation in perspective.

Their wedding had been a particularly private one and none of their friends and acquaintances was there. Back at home, none of his friends and co-workers could therefore vouch that they had observed the blushing bride. For this reason, curiosity would not let his co-workers allow them to go free. Since they did not witness the ceremony, they wanted to celebrate it with them. Johnny was the best boss they had ever met and he was one of them. He played with them, he ate with them and he mingled fully with them. To him, everyone contributed one way or the other to the success of the company and for that reason none was more important than the other. No other Chief Executive Officer would mingle with his workers that way. That was why each person always strived to put in his or her best.

As for this brand new idea of conjugal union, these workers believed that he was going to enjoy it. He used to be the most eligible bachelor in town and it was almost getting late for him. They were sure that he was going to enjoy it because of what they had observed thus far. The lady that had just spirited him away from the bachelors market looked more than well mannered. Apart from that, she was particularly beautiful and soft spoken. She spoke in a voice that most of them described as heavenly, though they most likely have never heard any voices from heaven before. She was as graceful as she looked elegant and she glowed in her loveliness. If good looks were the parameter to go by, she was surely going to make him very happy and vice versa. He was equally good looking.

Her curvaceously exquisite and delightfully delicate features were carried in a gorgeously dainty manner. That made her a complete glamour to behold. Pleasingly shapely, her good figure and ravishingly sublime comeliness has made her a thing of beauty or piece of art. She was the type that Venus or Aphrodite would be jealous of. In other words, she was a cutie whose lovely and well—polished pulchritude had turned her into a radiant and dishy morning star. She had become the object of all their eyes.

They wanted her to be part of them and they adored her. This was part of the reason why they could not see why a wedding party would not be in order. They had vowed to organize one for their boss and his wife and it was going to be a bash. It was going to be an unprecedented party in that area.

It was the president of the worker's union who was sent to Johnny. He was to present their plan to him. They knew their boss very well, and they were sure that his being very modest would make him disagree. If there was anyone who could convince him, it was going to be that president:

"Good morning sir." He greeted as soon as Johnny opened the door for him in his house.

"Oh it's you Frank. Come in. I hope there is nothing serious happening. I am not used to seeing you here unless something is amiss. Is there going to be a strike?"

"No sir."

"Come to the den and have a drink."

"Okay sir." He followed their beloved boss into his inner sitting room where they each poured out a head of whisky from the bar. It was not till he took the first satisfying sip of the whisky that he introduced the topic that brought him there, though in a roundabout manner:

"How is madam?"

"She's fine." Replied Johnny.

"And how was your honeymoon?"

"Couldn't be better."

"We didn't see that coming."

"Neither did I. It just happened."

"We are all excited for you."

"Well, thank you very much."

"Sir, I actually came to tell you that we held a general meeting yesterday. All the workers, with no exception, agreed that we should hold a party for you. They were afraid that you might not agree, and that was why they mandated me to present the case to you."

Johnny remained silent for about a minute in deep thought before he replied:

"If the union had reached that decision, then who am I to refuse them. My guess is that I have no choice."

"You do. We at least need your blessings to go ahead."

"How do you intend to raise the money for that? I hope it would be something within your means. If I remember very well, we did not have much in our coffers by the time I left on vacation."

"We asked for donations and within the hour we had much more than we would ever need."

"Good gracious!"

"They all love you and everyone was eager to express it."

"I hope it's not just that they simply want to have a party."

"Trust me. It is not that."

"In that case all I can say is that you should go ahead, though with only one condition."

"Which condition, sir?"

"I have to make my own contribution, after all it is my party, but apart from that, it is our party."

"In that case we will accept the money."

"Thanks."

"No, it is for me to thank you all."

It was as if it all happened at the same time and in the twinkle of an eye. That very evening, the stage was set for the show. It was going to start as a buffet dinner and for that they had hired a famous chef. They were going to provide a lot of food and drinks for everyone. Two live bands had been hired right away as if it was an emergency and there was going to be a lot of dancing. Each of the bands had been paid extra to abandon their previous gigs and attend to them. They were the two most popular bands in town.

There was one aspect of the party that he had to exclude though. They had planned to have a belated bachelor's party for him, in arrears as they put it. The ladies were also planning a spinster's eve for Joy. According to Frank, the workers had insisted that they were the final rites due to all escapees from single life. They did not see why any of them should miss it. One of them had insisted that it was like the graduation ceremony to mark the end of bachelorhood and spinsterhood. Those were the only parts of the party that had to be shelved.

Johnny and Joy did not waste time that evening as they got ready for the impromptu party. The stage had been set up at record time. All the workers were there and within an hour everything was ready and they all went home to prepare for the bash too. Joy had managed to succeed in fishing out her best party dress for the evening. For Johnny, it had to be the very same tuxedo that he wore for their wedding ceremony.

Unfortunately however, he was forced to rush both to the dry cleaner's for an emergency job. This was due to an unforeseen event that overtook them. Both clothes were laid out on the bed when suddenly that fire within them got kindled. That animal instinct had taken over their sense of reasoning as they threw caution to the winds. Desire for each other could have been a description of what had taken place, or maybe longing for each other, but neither phrase could quite describe what it really was. They yearned for each other and they had wanted each other to that point of infatuation. As they looked at each other, it was obvious that lust had become a complication from the love they had for each other.

The unbridled fury of this their desire for each other was so out of hand that they hugged, embraced and smooched as if they had not seen each other in more than a millennium. Within seconds, and as if by a miracle, their clothes were off on the floor and he was already caressing her breasts. They felt particularly full and velvety and he could not imagine why. Maybe it was the lust that had made him appreciate them more. Her nipples responded accordingly. They stood Up right away, with each hardening to quite a tough nut. Lots of rashes or maybe Goosebumps that were equally hard immediately came up all around the two nipples. They were localized mainly within the more pigmented areas around them. She closed her eyes to savor the touch of his hands and he in turn was lost in happiness for her happiness.

She was already behaving as if she was high on something, or intoxicated, when she held one of his hand and directed it further down. He did not try to disappoint her as he slid it all the way down to somewhere between her legs. He immediately began to caress that erotic zone. She immediately took up one leg to the edge of the bed in order to give him better access to the vital area. Each time his fingers moved in their measured strokes, she would jerk as if he was tickling her. At times it looked as if she had been shocked by electricity.

They were each so hot on each other that they fell onto the bed. She immediately took hold of his throbbing phallus and directed it right into her inner wet warmth. Each of them was by now panting wildly for breath. She let it slide all the way in. It was at the same moment that his sixth sense started giving him that premonition that an eruption was about to take place. She felt it too, but her own was already happening.

She shouted wildly as she climaxed and climaxed again, but she could not even hear her own voice, neither did she know that she was shouting. It was not in any specific language. It was at that very moment that his own came. He felt his ejaculate shoot deep into her in sizzling spurts. She felt its warmth as it raced all through into her and she even came some more. They jerked and banged into each other for a few minutes with each sweating profusely.

It was only after they had returned to their respective senses that they realized that they were right on top of their party dresses. Both dresses were wet with sweat and a few other unknown bodily fluids. If it had been any other couple, they would have found it horrifying or even mortifying. For these two love birds it was not so. They stood there looking at each other and then burst into laughter at what mess they had done when they were carried away.

Johnny then took the clothes and rushed off to the dry cleaners place. It was a rush job and he paid for it. He waited while the man took care of their clothing. Within an hour, he was back home with all the clothing in prime condition. He instantly hung them up to avoid any further unforeseen mishaps.

By six in the evening the arena not far from their house was already teeming with people. They were all workers from his office—The Exposition Computer Chips Industry. Johnny was their Chief Executive Officer. It was going to be the type of party that one could never forget. It was to mark the triumphant entry of their chief executive officer into the matrimonial league. A few were celebrating his loss. This was his loss from the group of eligible bachelors. He used to be the most eligible amongst them. The party was going to be a blow out by all standards.

Chairs and tables were arranged on either side of the open arena while on either end was a stage for the musicians.

Johnny had never been seen as a skirt chaser as such, and so they were not surprised that he got married. By half past six, the master of ceremony came back from their house to announce that all they were waiting for now was for the guest of honor to arrive. The guest of honor was taken as Johnny together with his new wife. It was barely a minute after that before they came out hand in hand from their house. They were welcomed with a standing ovation and ear slitting applause.

Johnny and Joy looked resplendent in their respective attires. Johnny was masculine and handsome at the same time. It was for this reason that most of the female workers there had a sort of crush on him. He looked virile and he looked strong. He was the type that could be referred to as a real man—a macho man. He was one heck of a man, quite broad shouldered and manly in every sense of it. Above all, he was a perfect gentleman.

As for Joy, her femininity was obvious from her party gown. It was a full length party dress made from a mauve silk material. Her curvy shape was made more obvious by the design of the dress. She looked very lady-like in every sense of it. This effeminate and nascent woman of the house was the epitome and undisputed ambassador of members of the fair sex. She was beautiful, she was pretty and she was all that.

They took dainty steps as they came to the arena to a table set at the center of one of the sides for them. The master of ceremony was their usher. As soon as they sat down, he cleared his voice and announced what they had come there for.

They had come there, according to him, to celebrate the loss of their Chief Executive Officer. He explained that he had always been with them no matter where they were. Now, however that he has a better half at home, he was going to be absent from them attending to his home. He had been stolen by the lady who was sitting next to him. He even likened what had happened as kidnapping with consent. To him, it was that pretty lady by his side that had kidnapped their boss. He did not however fail to point out that it was not her fault. He asked them to take a good look at her. He asked them whether it would not be total insanity for one to refuse to be kidnapped by her. They all sided with him.

He jokingly reminded them that though many of them might be wishing that she should kidnap them too, it was already too late. He then asked them whether there was any one present there who did not think that it was a clear and undisputed case of kidnapping. One person took up his hand to indicate that he did not think so. They were already agog with laughter and that only triggered off more laughter. She was a beauty without equal and she was a kidnapper. Rather than give the man who took up his hand to tell them why he did not agree, he turned to Johnny:

"Sir, could you tell us how you popped the question?"

"Which question?" Johnny asked.

"Having wooed her, how did you ask her to marry you?"

"If I remember very well, we didn't really consider the popping of any question."

"But that is not possible."

"Read my lips: It didn't happen."

"Then how did you get married?"

"It just happened."

"I give up."

The laughter that followed this was uproarious and it came from either side of the isle. Joy on her part was new to this as she nestled very close to her man feeling all shy and smiling. The master of ceremony then announced that the dinner was ready and the drinks were in abundance. It was time to do justice to each of them. People then began to get up and it was only then that he reminded them that before then, there was going to be an introductory dance led by the guest of honor.

It was the band at the left end of the arena that started it all off. It was a very cool and slow soul music and the ideal one for that very moment. The couple stood up, moved slowly to the center of the arena and then held tight to each other. They hardly moved. That was exactly the rhythm of the music. They were not meant to move around. They simply swayed lightly in each other's arms till a little osculatory activity between them brought up applause from the crowd.

At that very moment, the band stopped and the other one took over. What came from that band was something in the Hip Hop genre and it was a popular tone. Johnny was not all that of a dancer, but Joy was something else. She let go of him before proceeding to show them what it was all about.

She initially took a couple of well measured, moderately fast and intricate steps. This was followed by the real dance. She shook and vibrated all her body in every given direction to the sound of the music. The vibrations started from her chest area and proceeded down to her legs. She then gyrated and shook in such a way that her breasts bounced up and down in unison to the sound of the music.

It was not long before she reached the height of her demonstration as everyone watched on spell bound. She stooped low and vibrated her derriere in a show me fashion. This was too much for the crowd. They stood up and applauded so loudly that the sound of the music could no longer be heard. With that it had become too much for them as everyone trooped to the floor and joined in the dancing. As for Johnny, he was very much an onlooker like the rest. One of the ladies confessed at the end that Joy was not just the life, but the soul of the party.

Just as most people were about to break sweat, the band stopped. It was this clue that gave away the band. It was a very good band. It was time for dinner. The master of ceremony reminded them of that. Excitement was written on every face there. There were tables set behind each band's stage and they were full of edible goodies. All one had to do was to go over and scoop as much of whatever he or she wanted and then go back to his, or her seat and do justice to it. Drinks were in abundance too.

There were various mouthwatering salads, fried fish, barbecued spare ribs, mutton boiled in spices to absolute tenderness, oyster tails and shrimps fried in extra virgin olive oil, rice, peas, spaghetti, various sources and more. At the end of each table was a smaller one with assorted table wines both white and red as well as bottles of fine Champagne.

After he had returned from war, Julius Caesar was quoted as having said: "I came, I saw and I conquered." The master of ceremony for this occasion had to put it in a similar phrasing at the end of the party: "I came, I ate and I drank." The soft music was on all the time that they ate and chattered. After a while some bar men started going around making sure that people had enough to drink. There were whiskies, cognacs and other brandies, gins, different beers—especially the Guinness stout since Johnny had an Irish blood in him and of course there were various non-alcoholic drinks.

In time it was beginning to show that many were beginning to get drunk as they chatted and gossiped. The hottest gossip however was obvious. It was on how beautiful their boss's wife looked.

It was now time for the dancing session to begin. The effect of the alcohol is that they were now fully uninhibited. For this reason they danced wildly in all latest moves, they laughed wildly and they sweated wildly.

As for Johnny, he was their boss and so it was only reasonable that he had a certain amount of decorum to maintain in their presence. For this reason, though he was never a good drinker as such, he never drank much. Joy followed the cue. They remained there and once in a while someone would come to congratulate and chat with them. Occasionally too, one guy or the other would excuse Joy for a dance. She always obliged.

There was an uproar at one stage. It was when one of the janitors was so drunk that he did the unthinkable. He came up to their table, went down on one knee, held out his glass of whisky, and proposed to Joy with that glass. People roared with laughter, not just that he was proposing to their boss's wife but also that he was able to do so with a glass of whisky instead of a ring. To make matters worse, as soon as he finished with his proposal, he fell forwards and passed out. In that spirit of camaraderie, two of their colleagues came forwards to help carry him out. Unfortunately, or probably as would be expected, they had hardly taken five steps while carrying him when all three collapsed into one pathetic heap of drunks. That was the spirit of the party and virtually everyone was drunk. The ones who were not were only less drunk.

It was a Friday night and so it did not really matter. The weekend had begun and they were not going to work the following day. Most of them were so drunk that they could not even remember where they were. One of them actually staggered over to Johnny's house and started banging on the door while shouting on his wife to open up for him. He actually lived in an apartment complex about half a mile away. He thought that he was already home. Incidentally his apartment was on the third floor of the building where he lived.

As had been mentioned earlier, Johnny was not exactly into the drinks, but then he had actually had a few himself. He was beginning to feel that he might get drunk too and so he excused himself and his wife from the party though it was already late. Joy had imbibed quite a bit herself and so as soon as she entered the house, she raced to the bathroom. There she had a very cold shower which calmed her down and brought her back to her senses. After that she changed to a fairly hot shower which sort of invigorated her. She finished with this and then dried up.

Johnny went in after she had come out and he followed the exact same ritual. When he came out he was ready to pass out for the night, but his better half had other plans laid out for him. He came out from the showers only to see her pacing about the room stark naked.

"What's the problem?" he asked, "you don't seem to have your nighties on and you are pacing the room."

"I know."

"And so why?"

"I came into this word naked and I just feel like being naked, is there anything wrong with that?"

"No, I guess not, but why don't you try to put on something?

"No."

"Okay, let me help you get you negligee."

"If you insist." She said this with a suggestive wink. She had already noticed him hardening up beneath the bath towel he had around his waist.

They were highly fond of each other. He relished the sight of her nakedness and she swallowed hard at the sight of that hardening beneath the towel. The longing was there for each other. She looked highly seductive, which was the effect she had planned for, and he lusted after her with all his heart. He thirsted and itched for her, but despite the fact that they had made love not long before the party, she was already famished. She wanted him badly. She hungered and pined for him.

They met each other half-way as they came towards each other and they did not need any rehearsal before going into action. His biggest predilection was that bulge under his towel. It was insistent on pushing off the towel and it finally embarrassingly succeeded in achieving that. Before he could catch up with the falling towel, it was already on the floor with his throbbing erection standing ram rod and stiff like an army sergeant in salute. She quickly reached for it and grabbed it.

By just grabbing it, he got so excited that he immediately began to wet her palms with some slimy stuff. He was already shaking nervously as his fingers homed in on that her orifice. They somehow managed to find themselves on the floor while she held on to that stiff rod as if she was afraid of falling off the floor if she let go. They were already down so there should have been no further fear of falling.

Predictably, he began to caress her clitoris as she began to jerk wildly in all given directions but one—away from him. He grabbed at it with two fingers, he robbed it, he pinched it and he caressed it all at once. Those were enough to make her deliver a couple of fluids right into his cupped palm before he feverishly introduced himself into her. It was clearly an involuntary action this time around. She shuddered at that and held on tightly with her legs around him, while moaning, sighing and grabbing the air wildly all at once. That was too much for him to bear.

The volcanic eruption that followed from each of them was of an indeterminate magnitude while their bodies produced its own earthquake. It was of such intensity that it could have simply tipped the Richter scale. The aftershocks that followed from each of them also tended to increase in intensity rather than decrease. This continued till it reached an apparent crescendo and then suddenly died off. They had once more climaxed together in perfect unison.

They were now down from that mountaintop and they were exhausted while sweating profusely. Each of them was as winded as the other as they lay down there on the floor, each too tired to even stir. They were not asleep, but they only lay there and watched the ceiling silently, maybe for lack of any other thing to do. It did not take long before they dosed off only to be awakened by the sound of a cock crowing in the early morning.

The party had come and gone and it was now Saturday morning. They were still there on the floor and it was time for them to plan and map out what they were going to do for the coming week. They were now one, and it was time for them to map out the role each of them had to play in the partnership or merger as their company's financial analyst preferred to call it. He often insisted that marriage was definitely the merger between two different individuals. Its aim was for them to exploit the merits and dampen down the demerits of each of them to produce an entity that would be better than each of them alone.

There were no obvious happenings on Saturday. Most of the workers took it as the day to recover from the party.

As for Johnny and Joy, they had earlier decided to keep an appointment with nature on Saturday and they kept to that appointment.

Very early in the morning, they awoke to the noise from their alarm clock and it was time to get ready. They packed a few things into a backpack and then drove off. It took just ten minutes for them to arrive at their destination. It was a car parking lot in the middle of nowhere, but it was the beginning of a hiking trail. The forest in this area was irresistibly thin and the weather cool to the point of being slightly nippy. There were well established trails through the forest, but they had decided to simply head in one direction for about five hours and then later retrace their steps. A compass was to be their guide.

It was barely daylight when they took off into the forest. It was only slightly misty. The sun had just reared its head from the eastern horizon and it looked as if it was smiling on the earth. Everywhere was still in those half-lights as her more powerful rays tried to overwhelm those from the fast receding moon. It was not yet strong enough for it to cast any shadows and most of the animals were still asleep or just about to go to bed as the case may be. It looked as if the sun was coming up to usher in new life to the earth. To make sure that the sun did not shine straight into their eyes, they decided to make it due west; and like the lovers that they were, they took off hand in hand. They had decided to take it very easy. In other words, they simply strolled through the forest in total disregard to the trail itself.

The dew was barely there on the trees and it was not heavy enough for the drops to fall to the ground though everywhere was wet. One bush baby gave a convincing cry and that marked the end of the night marauders. It was a nocturnal animal, and if not for the fact that the cry came from deep within the forest they would have sworn that it was an actual human baby that was crying. It was just about to go to bed.

Some bats came flying by in a furious manner. They were already late getting home. They must have spent most of the night foraging for food and were now heading back home. They could very easily see their home. It was one tall tree not too far away. Their cacophony had betrayed their abode. They were going to spend most of the day up that tree hanging upside down.

Then that lovely smell of musk! It wafted straight into their nostrils. That was the first sign that a musk deer was around. Then came a ruffle from a nearby clump of shrubs and they decided to take a look. Sure enough there she was. A trap had caught her on one of her hind legs and she struggled to escape as soon as she saw them, but it was to no avail. A trapper was going to get happy latter on and it would not be right for them to try to set her free. The hunter was probably going to have some meat on his dinner table or to sell, but more importantly, some perfumers were going to pay him quite some money to possess the glands from where the odor came.

They had come out for the hike just at the correct time. It was when the animals were just changing their baton in their relay race. The night or nocturnal animals had just returned from the race to find food all through the night and the baton had just been handed over to the day time animals. It was as if the sideline umpire had just rung the bell to announce their arrival at the home stretch. All hell suddenly broke loose and the forest went wild with noise.

At first it was the birds. They were the first to make their presence known. They chirped, they twittered and they sang; and it was all in happiness at the arrival of a new day. Their voices came in various tones, some were nice to hear but others were totally disagreeable and disturbing to the ears. A lonely owl then hooted. It could have been her last for the night as she tried to retire. Maybe it was a warning call to other animals that she was about getting ready for a daytime hunt. Most of the birds stopped their noise and watched out for her. They wanted to be sure that she was not planning on an early morning hunt which was possible if she had spent a disappointing night.

A lot of termites were flying around and the birds had a field day feeding on them. The birds dived and swooped around in various daunting acrobatic maneuvers as they caught up with and snatched most of the termites on the wing. These termites were not just a welcome food windfall for them; they were also delicacies for humans who were after them as well. Some of the birds had come out rather too early but it was all for good course. They were after the fat—laden termites.

A crazy finch was actually so daring that it literarily plucked a termite off Joys head. The termite had come seeking refuge on her hair when the daring Finch swooped down and delicately plucked it off her hair and then immediately made it back up into the skies. It must have swallowed its catch while still flying since it could be seen chasing another termite.

As the sun began to rise higher into the skies, more and more birds began to appear. Many of them had started hopping from branch to branch. The younger ones rather than chase after the now few termites chose to play by chasing after each other. A couple of the birds had already had their full and were now resting as they perched on a nearby electric high tension wire. Both Joy and Johnny had stopped to watch what was happening. They loved to watch the birds in action.

A canary perched on a nearby branch as it began to belt out her tune. It was a high pitched intricate song from a throat that had rested well through the night and as fresh as it could get. Her renditions echoed through the entire forest far away. Within seconds there came a reply from another canary to announce her territory. Each of them had her own peculiar anthem as they called out on each other. She looked very tiny from where she perched on the highest branch of the tallest tree in the vicinity from where she rendered her songs. Joy and Johnny enjoyed the songs as they took photographs of that avian aria.

There was a large area that was largely clear of trees. It could have been a natural clearing or it could have been the result of human logging. At this time of the year it was full of various wild flowers. They were of various colors, shapes and sizes and of course the fragrance from that field was very enticing. They were there after about two hours due west and bees were everywhere around the flowers. Joy commented that she still marveled at how such tiny insects could produce the large amounts of honey in the market. They were terribly busy insects as they collected not just the nectar for their honey, but also pollen.

The bees were not the only visitors to the flower fields. Many other insects were also there, but the most prominent were the butterflies that came in more than many colors and sizes. They used their long proboscis to suck nectar from the flowers as they perched ever so delicately on them. They were a spectacle to behold as they flew and rode the winds like very flimsy kites from one flower to another.

They were gentle, harmless, noiseless and lovely. They fly without the slightest sound and at times it would seem as if they were tipsy, maybe tipsy after getting drunk from the nectar, if that was possible. In other words they seem to fly about in a sort of sleepy manner as they flirt with the flowers.

A small wild cat sat on a tree stump not too far away from there licking her bloody paws. She looked very happy and contented and they knew that she had just had a nice meal. She must have caught up with a rodent that was making it home late from its night foraging. They knew that her next move might be to lie down and sleep it off while letting the meal digest a little bit.

There were many other insects around, including the very tiny ones that they could not see very easily. They were however felt more than the rest. If not for the insect repelling bands that they wore, they would have surely had a lot of insect stings. They hovered around them but never really alighted on them. They could however hear some mosquitoes. They seemed to be complaining about the repellant. It separated them from their food.

Their attention was soon diverted to a hummingbird that appeared on the scene. It was a very tiny bird and it came to feed from a flower that was growing on a dead tree trunk. They could see the bird, but her wings remained invisible. The wings beat so fast that they were invisible to the human eye. Any other bird or even insect would perch to taste the nectar. No way! Not this hummingbird. It hovered over the flower and then stood still in the air as its long beak and tongue found their way into the funnel-shaped flower. It sipped the nectar and then flew away. It was the grand master of the air and flying.

There was so much to see and time went by very fast. Though it was almost nippy in the morning, it had become an overwhelmingly steamy mid-morning. They were already on the trail for over four hours and the sun was fast heading for the overhead position. It was hot and humid and they could not perspire, but sweat was in abundance. Fortunately they had a lot of water with them and they sipped the water as they went along. The humidity had made it a tiring adventure and so they decided to rest under a huge tree before heading back.

The tree was a huge umbrella tree which cast a lot of shadow. It was as cool as they had expected when they got there. There was a slight breeze and they could see a lot of shadows there created by light that filtered through the foliage. The shadows seemed to dance around in indeterminate pantomimes to soundless music. They seemed to dance even more and flip around whenever the breeze ruffled through the leaves and branches. Johnny even tried to imagine that they talked and gossiped in their silent voices, maybe about them.

He nearly confirmed this theory when a nearby whistling pine added its voice to the scene. He even went as far as to imagine that it was whistling in a cat call at Joy, most likely for her beauty. It must have however just responded to a slight gust of wind that just went by.

They were not the only ones that were interested in the shade. A couple of animals were there too and they made off as soon as they approached. The only ones that did not seem to care at all about the shade were a couple of lizards. They were basking in the full sun. Most of the animals were also feeling the heat and so the noise had died down. Everywhere was now silent and it was already way after midmorning. It was only the steamy humid heat that could achieve that. The silence seemed to echo through the entire forest in a resounding eloquence. The silence was so obvious that they even began to feel sleepy.

As they sat there for a breather, a group of monkeys swung through the tree and noisily jumped to another. Embarrassingly however was one particular monkey. She sat there on a bough and looked at them very intensely. She watched them with unwavering intensity and it all seemed very queer to them. It was only when they decided on a snack that it all dawned on them. She must have been a monkey that had been reintroduced to the wild.

As soon as the sandwiches appeared it became obvious why she was there. She alighted from the branch and continued to watch them while sitting on the ground not too far away from them. Joy was excited as she realized what it was all about. She offered her half of her sandwich and she quickly but timidly snatched it from her and went back to eat it. They ate together and at the end Johnny offered her his coca cola which she drank too.

At the end they got up and bade her goodbye. She reluctantly jumped back into the tree and then sped away in search of the rest of the troupe. They had embarked on a nature trek and they had enjoyed it a lot. They were more than satisfied, not minding the heat and humidity. By the time they got back to where they had parked their car, they were each completely exhausted. They rested for a few minutes in the air conditioned car recounting what points of interest they had seen before heading back home. It was already late afternoon to early evening when they got home.

As soon as they got home each person dived into the shower for a quick one. It was cold water shower. It was to help them cool down from the hot steamy day, wash off the sweat and get rejuvenated. They came out of their bathrooms at the same time, and as soon as they beheld each other, that spark began to fly once more.

As they saw each other scantily dressed, if dressed at all, it was instant attraction as they flew into each other's arms. They immediately began to kiss. It was one of those very passionate ones with their lips tightly stuck together. Each person's tongue made forages into the other's mouth searching around passionately, maybe for the source of that elixir of love that was on them. This osculatory activity continued for a while with their lips still tightly interlocked. It was however eventually time for Johnny to extricate himself and try something else.

He gently swung her around so that she backed him. She had been eagerly awaiting that. He then embraced her from the back with his palms over her breasts. They were massive palms and her breasts were just a perfect fit for them. He squeezed gently and caressed them with Her nipples protruding from between some of his fingers. That gave him the opportunity to mess around with them, nestled in-between those fingers, all at the same time. As he rubbed them, those telltale nipples suddenly betrayed her innermost emotions. They got bigger and very stiff.

He knew that she was enjoying it and he felt very happy at her happiness. She arched backwards to let him get the best out of the adventures of his hands. She had surrendered her entire body to him. It was at this juncture that he let one hand slide further down, and she shivered in anticipation. She knew what those fingers were capable of. He lowered it all the way to in-between her legs and she simply exploded with excitement. She had made every possible effort not to show her emotions, but she could no longer control it. She let out a couple of sighs of resignation as his finger hit that her erotic zone.

As soon as he began to fiddle with and tease her now stiffening clitoris those sighs blossomed into moans of passion. They were very soft moans at first, but they soon increased in both loudness and frequency. His fingers played and danced a series of pantomimes in that entire area. Some ventured inside the vagina while others stuck to activities outside it. She arched and shook every which way as a series of premature orgasms made their presence known. She sighed and moaned both at once. She was already dripping wet and he knew that she was more than ready for him. As for himself, his penis was now ram rod erect and throbbing painfully. Above all, it was now dripping whatever juice it was, like a raging bull itching for a fight.

It was only then that he gently scooped her up and gingerly laid her on the bed. She had waited patiently though eagerly for that. He laid her on her back and climbed on top of her both at once. She was in too much of a hurry as he was not fast enough. She immediately took command. She took hold of that throbbing equipment with feverishly shaky fingers and quickly inserted it into her vagina all by herself. Part of the reason why she had to do it by herself was however because she wanted a good grip and feel of that enormous organ that had always given her total excitement, enjoyment and satisfaction.

As for Johnny, he could not bear it any longer and he started to pump right away. She held tight on to him, gripping even tighter with her legs as she responded to each of his movements in a reciprocal manner. It all took place in full harmony, though with a sort of reckless abandon. The thrusts then increased both in frequency and intensity and it was at this stage that she began to speak in those weird tongues. They were various and diverse—the tongues that is—but none of them could understand what she said, not even she herself. In other words she was actually speaking in tongues. They were surely the tongues of Aliens, despite the fact that none of them had ever heard nor seen an Alien before. It was eventually pinned on Aliens from a neighboring solar system.

This continued till it got to a sort of apparent crescendo At which time and stage she let out a wild scream. He was almost alarmed, but then he quickly realized that it was a satisfying type of scream that was triggered off by a certain upheaval that had just begun deep down within her. It actually took place involuntarily to mark the arrival of one of those unprecedented orgasms. It was so intense that it could easily be equated to a volcanic eruption, and it made her to literally loose control.

Her internal vaginal walls were already contracting and relaxing in intense and wild waves. They took place in such a manner as to suck in anything within her further in into her, both penis and ejaculate alike. All her skeletal muscles had tightened to an unbelievable rigidity as she shook like one having a convulsion.

Johnny felt it and he knew what was going on. This was mainly because his own was starting at the same time too. There was that premonition that something big was about to happen as he began to stiffen all over. He then began to grunt like a male pig in heat. All his muscles began to stiffen as well; especially those smooth ones lower down. It was a completely involuntary activity. He stiffened and tightened and only one thing was in his mind at that moment—what was going on down there.

Each of them had become single minded. They did not exactly recognize the presence of one another. All that mattered was whatever it was that was happening down there. It was like a volcanic eruption and an earthquake that had tipped the Richter scale taking place both at once from the same epicenter.

His ejaculate pumped out with all ferocity and speed into her. She willingly and hospitably accepted as well as welcomed them with equal intensity. Everything he had seemed to have come out of him and everything that came out went into her. Before they knew it, everything that was happening ended abruptly just as it had all begun. It had been very intense, it had been totally satisfying and they were each completely fulfilled.

They had been exhausted by that nature hike and now this! They were both panting and out of breath and neither of them knew what happened next. They only managed to wake up some twelve hours later each as naked as they were when it all started or rather as naked as they were at birth. That was their story and how they had spent their Saturday.

On Sunday however, they attended service at the interdenominational church that was located just outside the company's premises. This was a truly interdenominational church. It was the product and brain child of their quality control analyst. He had often described himself as a freewheeling pastor. He was an ordained Roman Catholic Priest before quitting the order, and he had two doctorate degrees. He had his first degree in mathematics, his masters in statistics and electrical engineering and a doctorate in Computer engineering. He later went in for a doctorate in Philosophy.

He had succeeded in convincing most of the workers there that they should work for the company for five days, do their own personal chores for one day and then rest on the seventh as God did. He made up his own mode of service. This included inputs from various other religions so that he could accommodate all. There was one Jewish family amongst them and he once tried to convince them to come to church on Sundays. He had assured them that by the time God created the earth there was no writing and no calendars. Man was created after that. No one was therefore sure of which the seventh day was not to talk of which the first was. Adam and Eve obviously had no idea of that.

It was man that invented the calendar, and what is commonly used now is even the Roman calendar which came much later than many others. It would therefore be alright to worship Him on a Sunday. Though Sunday was the day the early pagan Romans worshiped the Sun god, Christianity chose to go with it. The day did not matter, it was the concept that did. Take it as the seventh. Some would take Friday and others Saturday. Funny enough, according to our calendar, Sunday is the first day of the week. Why Christians rest on this first day remains a puzzle. God rested on the seventh but they remember it by resting on the first day instead.

Some aspects of the order of service were from the Christian religion, some from pure Judaism and others from Islam. Any Hindu would recognize some aspects of their practice and he was there as the chief priest.

This was where the two newlyweds went that Sunday morning. Johnny had an open mind when it came to religion and everything that went on there was acceptable and familiar to him. For Joy, it was odd. According to the chief priest, worshipping God from and with all your heart was more important that how it was done. That Jewish man had insisted that the mode of worship mattered a lot till the priest asked him one simple question: "Why is it that in Judaism you no longer sacrifice animals in the synagogues?" It was supposed to have been a direct order from God to do so at the altar. That was when he stopped protesting, for according to the priest, practices change with time and that was one of the changes, just like his own.

At the end of the service they all trooped outside, and one could notice that climate of camaraderie with them. The friendliness, the familiarity and the jollity that was obvious overwhelmed Joy. They formed a closely knit group. The bond was that friendly work environment. They were like a clique of brothers and friends rather than coworkers and that had translated and resulted in an extraordinary work environment where everyone wanted to contribute his best.

Each person there knew every other person and going to work felt more like attending a social gathering by members of the same group. That was the type of work environment that Johnny had created. They talked, they gossiped, they laughed and they giggled as they went outside at the end of the service. This congenial atmosphere was in itself simply palpable and it was like a merrymaking environment. To improve on these feelings, entertainment was provided at the end of the service. These entertainments were usually sponsored by volunteers and they never lacked these. Each would always try to outdo the other.

For the day in question, it was two female workers that teamed up to provide the entertainment which usually took place at the rear of the church on their way out. It was essentially a bash once more. It looked as if the merriment from the other night was just about to continue. They were treated to spit barbecued tender lamb meat, spare ribs marinated and boiled to absolute tenderness, salads, various non-alcoholic drinks, quail eggs and sweet seedless grapes as well as water melons.

Joy was rather too impressed. She had insisted that they were not just coworkers. To her, they were a family of brothers and sisters working together in the same place, and she was into them right away. As for the female workers, she was already on first name basis with most of them, as well as with the wives of many of the male ones.

After the service, Johnny drove into the town to visit as much of it as they could and visit all areas of tourist interest. The company with its workers had formed a closely knit village some ten miles away from the city to which it belonged. This sprawling city had a population of well over three million. It was a really big city.

Just like most big cities, it had an area for the rich and middle class which was around its perimeter. The inner city was of course dominated by the slums for the poor and homeless. The city actually was born out of five industries that started there. The computer chip industry was a late entrant and so it was built way off the city. All the workers there lived all around the industry. The houses there were all built by the industry and accommodation was free for all its workers. It was for this reason that the rest of the city regarded them as people who lived in paradise. In fact the area was popularly called 'paradise cove.'

They visited different areas of the city, and by the time they got back it was already way beyond afternoon. As soon as they got home, they began to undress since they were still in their church attires. As had been usual with them, which was enough to throw them off balance, as it were. Caution was not part of their consideration. They were at home and they were married so everything had to take place carelessly. They felt free and they lived free. They were each pleased to see one other stripping into nudeness, and they relished watching each other in that form.

She was oftener than not intoxicated by just watching him strip and one could feel the electricity in the air as they surreptitiously watched each other. Sparks were already flying in all given directions. They were each now bent on satisfying the other and in being happy in each other's happiness They were already beginning to approach each other, and by the time they met in the middle of the room, though looking very delicately lascivious, she was more like a lioness ready to pounce. The fury of the lust that had taken over her senses had already turned her into a pleasure seeking as well as pleasure giving fiend complete with red dilated pupils. She literarily pounced on him as they met.

He went down on his knees and tried to give her pleasure by cunilingus. It was new to him. With his mouth now firmly planted around her orifice, he began to search all around and within her vagina for I know not what. He licked as he tickled away. He also teased that her hot spot with his tongue and she responded. It felt ticklish, but then it was pleasurable, maybe too much so, and she never wanted him to stop. She was so wild that she grabbed his head and tried to force it so close that it looked as if she wanted it to go right inside her. That almost smoldered him out of his breath as he struggled for a breath of fresh air. She was already too excited to care. She hissed, she grunted and she even cried aloud whenever he nibbled at that tiny hot stiffness. It was the ultimate perception of pleasure.

She was well aware of what he was doing down there but she was about to lose consciousness as she tried very hard to repress that urge to force his head right inside her, if she could. It was going to be worth it to at least try though she knew that it was not going to be possible. It was his first time of trying that on her and her responsiveness to it was unprecedented. It was so pleasurable that she ran short of both words and sounds.

It was not long before she suddenly pushed his head away from between her legs. He thought that he had done something wrong, but it was not so. It was only to give her the opportunity to lie on her back in other to give him the opportunity to come into her. Each of them was now in a hurry and shaking with anticipation. They seemed inexplicably nervous as he hurriedly let himself into her. He stuck it all the way in and she began to gasp and wriggle her derriere. Her sex drive was at its height, just like his own, and each of them feverishly desired the others flesh.

No one was very sure of the chemistry of his erection. What was obvious is that within a matter of seconds this unplanned concupiscence was about to get to its climax and possible end. Mysteriously, the more they met the shorter it took for each of them to achieve orgasm and the more perfect it became.

Just then, all his muscles began to tighten and hers responded in the same manner. This could have been due to the pure chemistry between them. His organ sort of seemed to grow miraculously in length and girth both at once, and it felt as if it was about to burst. Somehow or the other, she seemed to have both anticipated and felt it happen. It was however all a feeling as excess blood rushed into it to give it enough energy for the approaching climax. Then came that combined and synchronized orgasm! She had experienced quite a few of them already, but this was the big one! Holly molly!

The floodgates of his seminal reservoir had just been let open but the dam had already broken down. It squirted out its fluid at supersonic speed and flooded her inner caverns, just at the same time as all her vaginal musculature began to contract wildly in all imaginable directions. She then grabbed his buttocks and held it tight in an attempt to get him to go deeper into her. Suddenly he heard her shout: "MOORE!" She shouted thrice before her voice began to die down. It was one of the steamiest love episodes that they had gone through so far. It left them dog tired as all the eruptions and demands died down before they collapsed into each other's arms completely windless and weary. She had slightly more energy than him as she was still able to speak haltingly in-between pants. She weakly asked him not to withdraw it even though it had gone flaccid.

It was one of the most brutal and grueling love-making episodes that they had been through so far. They were completely burnt out and the carpet on which they lay was wet with their sweat and a few other bodily fluids. Those did not matter anyway. They were almost immediately off to that dream world.

It was from a latter account that it was learnt that they were each lying there on the floor dreaming of each other. Though they dreamt of each other, they were not too sure that it was of the other. In fact they were not too sure of what they dreamt about though they were sure that they dreamt. In other words they were each too tired to remember what they dreamt about or maybe even to dream at all.

Johnny was the Chief Executive Officer of the company and for that reason he was always travelling about. It goes with that position. The problem that came with this is that he had just got married. It meant that he will be away from his new wife most of the time. She was going to miss him a lot too so early in the marriage. It was his duty to generate customers and funds for the company and he was very good at that. It has also come to be his new duty to generate happiness for his wife. It was in this second area that he was going to have problems.

He had a super-executive Lear jet at his disposal for these journeys which took him to almost everywhere around the world. To compensate for this shortcoming, he travelled with her on occasions, depending on what the mission was going to be. From her behavior now, it was obvious that she was already beginning to miss him. He, on his part, tried his best to make sure that he wasn't away too often and for prolonged periods of time. As a bachelor he could be away for weeks on end, but now the longest he had been away was for three days.

They finally agreed that he had to find something for her to be doing. That way she might not find it too lonely whenever he was away. Educationally, Joy had her first degree in personnel management before a masters in sociology. She worked as a personnel management officer for a university from where she got a post graduate diploma in Journalism. This was the profession that exposed her to the world as it were, and she loved it—the world that is.

It was while working as an investigative journalist for a news agency that she found herself thrust into an entirely new profession. The news agency was small and hitherto unknown until she stepped in. She was thrust into the limelight when a scandal arose in the church and she was chosen to cover it. A priest had been directly tied up to a murder. The law enforcement agencies went into crime scene reconstruction, and he came out as the only and obvious suspect. After going through their report, Joy was convinced that they were wrong. There were unanswered questions.

The priest had lodged in a hotel with an escort. As if that was not scandal enough, the escort's body was found in their room in the hotel some hours after he left. She had been in the room with him for three days before his departure. According to the police that particular escort was well known to them. She was in the habit of demanding more than had been agreed to from her clients. They were convinced that she must have done the same thing again. According to the autopsy report, she had died just at about the same time that the priest left. It was therefore obvious that she had demanded a lot of money, or even threatened to blackmail him and so he, in a fit of rage and fury, strangled her. That was their final report, and it was a straightforward case.

According to their records, the escort agency had charged the priest thirty thousand dollars for the three days service. Tips were however to be negotiated between him and the girl. For the agency, payment is usually done before service and he had actually paid long before the service. He was their regular customer. It was however his first time with that particular girl. She was fairly new there. The police knew that she had demanded for a lot of money and she had actually threatened to blackmail him if he did not pay up. They knew this because all the rooms there were bugged. There was a suspected terrorist who lodged there very often and the intelligence community did not want to miss any conversations from him.

The girl had demanded for twenty thousand dollars as tips. He had only six thousand left with him and she had insisted that it was nothing. The twenty was what she wanted. She had intimated that she would not have asked for that if not for the fact that she had a project at hand. She insisted that she needed the money urgently too. Somehow or the other it was at that stage that the bugging devise stopped recording.

To the police, it was obvious as to what had happened. He had detected the device and damaged it. He had finally killed her by strangling after that. He probably expected that no one would think of associating the crime with him since it was not probably going to be discovered till much later after he had gone. It was a cleaning lady that discovered the corpse barely an hour after he was gone. The lady had a date and so she was in a hurry to finish her work early.

Joy did not see it that way. Supposing another person had done that just as the priest was leaving, but who could that be? What was the project she had at hand? These were unanswered and the police were not interested. She therefore decided to start off with her own investigation. She was then still very young and pretty and it did not take long before she hit on the truth.

Unknown to anyone, this girl had a fiancée. She discovered that the girl had to generate a lot of money so that she and this boyfriend of hers could stand on their feet after they got married. The fiancée was in on her activities because she managed to convince him that nothing went on between her and her clients. She had explained to him that it was why she only went with priests who were celibate. They only 'leased' her from the company for her secretarial abilities, and they always slept apart in different rooms. He did not initially suspect anything wrong since she majored in secretarial studies and she had initially worked for a firm that had secretaries for loan.

The story looked alright on the surface, but Joy did not believe that the boy could have swallowed that story hook line and sinker. He was bound to investigate and try to find out more. As soon as she identified the fiancée, she shifted her investigation back to the hotel. Her brains were working at full throttle. They gave her access to their surveillance film database and she decided to see everyone that went in and out of the hotel within those three days. Her fiancée was there on each of those three days.

It was while trying to find out from where the priest got that large amount of money that her interest in money got kindled. Priests were known to be poor, otherwise there wouldn't have been that phrase: "as poor as a church mouse." Mind you this excludes the independent churches that were in general awash with money. In the case of this priest, it was obvious that the priests actually controlled the churches collections and only they could give account of how they were being used. There were church offerings, there were gifts, donations for various projects, and they were always in abundance. There were also donations from organizations as well as from various governments. These were all tax free.

It was like a trove of money that did not need being properly accounted for. The priests who controlled this money usually lived in affluence, but it was never very obvious. The priest in question could have very easily paid that girl the money, but he was a very frugal character. It was even possible that after the recorder stopped working, he had agreed to give her the money. It was also interesting to note that neither of them raised their voices during all this discussion and so the possibility of he committing that crime seemed to be very slim.

Now back to her fiancée, he was in the hotel barely thirty minutes before the priest left. To avoid suspicion, the priest always left some two to three hours before his escorts. That way no one would ever associate them with each other. She then decided to find out where her fiancée was at that moment when the priest left. She was sure that he had something to do with it.

She eventually got permission, from the hotel authorities to interview some of their workers. Privately she showed them the fiancées photograph one by one. The priest was in the sixth floor and so she interviewed every one that was there between the period that he came in up to an hour after that. Some of them had seen the man on occasions but none could remember having seen him that day.

At last one of the janitors said that she saw him that day. He said that he had come across him on the stairs on one other occasion climbing up. He had believed that he was one of their guests. He had seen him that morning coming out of the stairs door on the sixth floor and he could remember that it was when the clock on the wall struck seven o'clock in the morning. That was exactly ten minutes after the priest left. The difference that day was that he was sweating profusely and panting. It was obvious that he had run up the stairs.

From that, Joy came to conclude that he had seen the priest leaving with his luggage and so he ran up to pay her a surprise visit. That was the reason for the panting and there was the killer.

There was also another interesting and salient point. On the day that the priest checked in, he had been seen at the reception. He was there to give a call to his confessor. He was given the phone at the reception as well as the priest's name and room number. He also found out that the priest did not book for more than one room which automatically meant that he was using the same room with his woman. The receptionist did not recollect that particular incident but it was usual for people to come in to check up on visiting priests. In other words he had been stalking the two right from the beginning.

When she handed her report over to the news agency, they were excited with her result and they quickly handed it over to the police instead of broadcasting it. That was what saved that priest from being sentenced to life or more likely to death. He could have been executed for cold blooded murder. When her fiancée was arrested by the police and the evidence presented to him, he owned up that he was the person who killed her.

According to him, when he knocked on the door, the girl ran over and opened it thinking that the priest must have forgotten something and come back for it. She was in a see through negligee with no underwear at all. He had now seen what her secretarial duties were; moreover they were sleeping in the same room. He strangled her in his furry and left the hotel as he had come. He did not touch the money because to him, it was dirty money. He had done that while livid with anger at how she had betrayed him.

The judge eventually found the boy guilty after he was arraigned before him. He however took a little pity on him since it was done in anger after a betrayal some two weeks to their wedding. Rather than sentence him to death as was expected, he sentenced him to life imprisonment with the possibility of parole after serving hundred. He was twenty-two and everyone knew what that meant.

This investigation had helped Joy realize that there was a lot of money lying idle somewhere waiting to be rescued. It was money that belonged to no one in particular. It was lying there like holy water waiting for anyone who knew where it was to come in and dip his finger into it for a few drops. Uncannily like the holy water, it was lying there in care of the priests. It was money that did not exactly belong to anyone, that is technically speaking. It belongs to God. She was bent on going in and helping herself to it, and that was why and how she went into the escort business.

She did not go deeply into it like most of the other girls that got involved with that earliest of all professions. She was a very smart lady and when I say smart, I mean smart. She sought out the priest after everything had died down and introduced herself to him. Who else was that priest but that Bishop that later became her boyfriend. He was the priest in question and directly after that incidence he was elevated to the rank of Bishop. He however left the order to chase after the money by himself. He had been properly trained and he was now an expert and knew all the tricks of the trade. He was into church business and not into God's business. He was not there to win souls but to win money.

Joy was pretty and irresistible, and when the Bishop learnt that she was the journalist who literarily and singlehandedly saved his life, he vowed that he owed her and would pay back. That was how he came to lavish a lot of money on her. He was married all the while but it had now become official. It was a job that turned out to be so lucrative that what she made in a month was more than what she earned as a journalist in three years. He was her only serious client. The Bishop was a businessman. He was into church business, as had been pointed out before, which had become a very lucrative business and he was very good at it. He made tons of money, and it was all tax free.

There were many priests in this business or rather preachers. They were predominantly into the Church business as opposed to Gods business. They were mainly into making money. For them, the phrase 'as poor as a church mouse' was not applicable. They preferred the phrase: "My God is not a poor God." They were usually extremely busy—busy making money. Joy's journalistic mind had led her into peeping into the practices of a few of them.

There was one of them who was famed as a great healer. By the time Joy went into investigating him, she had at the back of her mind that saying that was popular with her Sunday school teachers as a child: "many shall heal in my name, but I know them not." She had seen this man perform healing miracles. Many miracles could be true since some of them could have been healed by their faiths, but she had come across one that was not quite a healing miracle. That had taken place when she saw that pastor heal a lame man during a crusade. Unfortunately for him, the patient was known to her. Both he and his friend who had been healed of blindness earned seven hundred dollars each that Sunday to fake their respective illnesses, and they had come from far away.

For one of them, it was a full time job, and he lived an affluent life by just being hired out to preachers for healing purposes, especially at far away crusades. At times he dressed as an old beggar and at times as a lady. According to him, he was just like any other actor, the only difference was that he did not live in Hollywood and his acting was live. In many instances, they were wise enough to make these healings far from home. Go back to bring a sick man to him and he is gone. For those who do it at home, whenever the healing could not take place then the sick man must be of little faith. Mind you this does not mean that there were no real healers.

She had come across one who had acquired some diabolical powers with which he healed. Those powers had come from a witch doctor. One was the daughter of a voodoo priest and she employed some of her father's powers to heal. For these two, they were using powers from the devil in the name of the Lord. There was actually one who had only graduated into becoming a faith healer. He used to be an unsuccessful itinerant magician.

With this trove of experience Johnny felt that it might be good for him to secure some position for her within the company. One of the workers actually campaigned from behind to make sure that she was employed when Johnny brought up the idea during one of their management meetings. She was eventually employed as the director of Personnel and Social services. Though he was in the know as to the application, her employment took place when he was away.

It was an easy job, but it kept her busy enough not to feel the incessant absence of her husband. She enjoyed it because it was a job that tapped into her field of study and professional training. It was very satisfying to her, mainly because she now looked at herself as having veered back to what she considered gainful employment. She had considered her venture into the world of the escort business as an irresponsible adventure away from reality, though it was very lucrative. She had also found herself thrust into an enviable position, a position that she had never imagined that she could attain in her life. This was indeed her true calling and she did put her soul into it. She gave it all that she had, and it yielded results.

The company boomed and its working environment became even more cordial with her presence. All the workers loved her and some actually swore that she was God sent. This helped to ease off a little bit on her feeling of partial marital abandonment. She was a very popular employee, if not for what she had achieved, then at least for her enviable beauty. Many admired her character and what she had achieved for them, but there were a few who loved her for her beauty and amongst these were a few unmarried ones.

It had been pure marital bliss and so far they were both still completely obsessed with each other. They also delighted in teasing one another.

It was a Sunday and they had decided to sleep off the entire day, if possible. It was already the crack of dawn, though it was not yet waking time, Joy was already up and about. She often delighted in standing by the rear window of the building at such wee hours to watch the placid sea behind their house. At this time it always looked very serene. Their house was built on the top of a cliff and that was how it came to overlook the ocean. From there one could always see a chain of small volcanic islands not too far away, and each of them was unique on its own.

These islands were technically uninhabited and people as well as any sight seers were free to go to any of them. The group was known as Traveler's Archipelago. It was while watching them from the window that morning that she remembered a rather long poem that she had come across in Johnny's study drawer by that window. It was the child of his imagination after he had visited a few of the islands in the group. It was also how the group got its name. It was titled: Traveler's Archipelago.

Traveller's Archipelago

Not far from the ocean, there they lie
Previously set from flowing lava—
All you see is worth the sight
Emerging from depths as deep as deep could be.

Far below from that bottomless sea
Often blue with billowing waves
Come undersea craters spewing fear
Through briny depths into abundant clouds.

Now mature many islands had formed
Leaving behind half-formed ones.
Their greeneries from nothing had come
Alive with most of the folia and fauna on earth.

Hills and mountains had come to be
Often high with challenging cliffs
That oftener still juts down the depthless sea—
And one could meander through their shores.

Atlantis or Pacifis, it's still a sea
And each closer to each had come to be;
Yet far they seem so far asea
As one must meander through their meandry shores.

Traveler's Archipelago!
A wanton disarray of fabled isles
Some small and bare, others big and rare
With some yet to break the surface.

Full of hazards the straights between them
As some craters are barely a fathom deep—
A hazard to unsuspecting jolly men
In this calm water that's a heaven for ships.

The islands were diverse in size and shape
Full of trees and shrubs and grasses,
Full of animals often curious in size and shapes—
Many in various stages of evolution.

The great trees with their breathing spikes—
Roots that jot from the water into the air;
Their nostrils above the low tide marks
Struggle with man for the air above.

The vines entwine their ravishing trunks
Clinging onto and suffocating the smaller trees
And cutting off the sun from the shortest shrubs
That thrive from far below.

Their fruits and flowers come from ravishing buds
While berries, drupes and all
Attract all the curious minds.
And they need none to help them move.

Various birds often in spectacular suits
Some of them small and others big
Chirp and peck at all the fruits
Eating and carrying some far away.

The chimps and all the monkeys
Do swing from bough to bough
Cheeks blown with assorted goodies
As they loot and eat the ripening fruits.

Many a rodent far below do have their fill
Picking and eating the crumbs that fall
Especially from the birds as they peck at will
Often shying away as snakes chance by.

Their droppings the beetles try to own
As the frogs and toads watch out for them.
The owls at night hunt for their own
As do the hawks and kites by day.

Travelers later do their own as well—
Not content with the delicious berries,
They kill and eat the animals as well-
A case of the survival of the fittest.

By the sandy shores unnumbered prints
Their owners unknown to us abound,
Since many chance by at night with those prints
As do others by daylight too.

Many had come but for to quench their thirst
At these banks that teem with fish
Of all types and shapes and weight
Each waiting for to be picked up at will.

Fully grown and heavy with hoods
The lizards closely hug the stony cliffs
As they eat the moss and stray foods
Or simply basking in the sun for warmth.

The travelers idly pick their choice
As they pass through these fertile straights
Where fish seem to wait to be caught and diced—
With many so heavy they break the lines.

Many unaware of what man is
Actually to their boats come to look
Especially along the yonder Hypnos pass
That was prior unnavigated by man before.

The beaches are so smooth and silky soft
With sands nascent from the earthly wombs
Palms with fruits that are barely husked
Could make a man to into oblivion melt.

Granite obelisks often here abound
Which like totem poles look out into the sea
To guard and ward off evil from this land
And impose some awe to all that pass.

Here the winds are steady but light—
Cool and mellowed they come
Seemingly from both the north and the south,
As they pantomime in their own dance of joy.

The sun timid but never loud
Gives heat that's neither hot nor cool,
As if they come from behind some fair weather clouds.
Though cloudless, these skies have always been.

Passing here over the cloudless deeps
Is more like invading the privacy of the heavens
And it is an experience that one gets and keeps;
For Mesmer could nothing further do to this.

Oftener cloudless than ever some clouds
Oftener rainless than ever some rains
The night though dark-less is somewhat dark
With lights that filter in from here and there.

Just as the stars are spangled above
So these islands are spangled beneath.
Just as the stars twinkle from far above,
So do these islands with their wind swept shores.

Many a sailor had wrecked their ships
While enjoying this sight at night.
Too many mates have fallen from their ships
Pulled by the powers of these enchanted isles.

Fairly deep into one of the craters
Where warm and sulfurous baths do exist
Nothing does change of he who recreates—
For it is the fountain of youth and warmth.

Many pass and wish to stay till 'morn
In this paradise on earth am told.
How I love to see this sight at dawn—
Travelers Archipelago—a heaven on earth.

This was an apt and vivid description of what these enchanting groups of tiny islands were. It also reflected a true account of their effect on the mind. That was exactly the effect that it had on Joy that very morning.

She was still there when a different but familiar scenario started to reintroduce itself. It was going to be a near reenactment of the ROYGBIV rainbow attire scenario. Johnny had seen her admiring that group of islands as he did some days before. He was however admiring her just as she did the islands. He had called out for her, but she was too rapt up in her admiration of those hypnotizing islands to hear his call. He therefore decided to go over to her. The fire was still there between the two of them and it was still burning ever fiercely. It was that fire of love.

The sunrise might have had something to do with their feelings. It was still very early into that shy peep of the day. It was still that period of half lights and half twilights when the very first blush of the morning could be seen only around the horizon. It came as a subtle bronze hue that looked more like her blush.

Together with the traveler's archipelago, that early morning blush had done a lot of justice to her beauty. Her full feminity was obvious against that backdrop. This was accentuated by the fact that she only had on a near ephemeral negligee which had changed her natural attractiveness to pure human magnetism. He was more than fully aroused and his sexual desires were at their peak. That animalistic mating instinct had taken over and he itched all over for her. His footsteps were what made Joy turn around as he approached her. She immediately saw what was in his eyes and she was instantly caught up in it too.

His masculinity was obvious. He was a beef-cake and one hunk of a man, as she often put it, and he appealed to her immensely. That was enough to push her off the edge. She was already in a hurry in pursuit of passionate pleasure. Intercourse with her husband had always been like an opiate trip to her. His touch was intimacy in itself and it was often more than enough to catapult her into that other realm and world. Just his sight alone would have been enough to turn her on and put her on fire.

Excitement was in the air and the thrill was obvious. Her heart fluttered in apparent and expectant excitation as that fire of love took over with all its furry. She embraced him, and without as much as a single word they hugged each other like long lost lovers. By the time they advanced to kissing, the frenzy and madness of love was already obvious.

It was an upheaval within each of them. This was caused by that whirlwind of desire which had come like a relentless tornado to stir up that fire beneath. They grabbed at each other in ecstasy. He went for her breasts, but she had no time for that. She had other plans. She quickly and feverishly redirected his adventurous hands to that area further down from where the heat seemed to be emanating. The longing for each other was beyond description as each wanted to be laid and without control too. She did not require any further arousal for his fingers were already within and around that erotic zone.

Her eyes were much glazed as she moaned and cried while looking unseeingly into the air. He had hit her soft spot. She yelled out for more while pushing him down to the floor and riding him as a cowboy on a rodeo practice. She immediately thrust his manhood into her now wet and awaiting womanhood. She rode feverishly. Each thrust, which was under her control, hit home and it was obvious from her face. At times it looked paradoxical or rather like an equivocation. Her face would look contorted as if she was in serious pain, but then she actually wanted more and she made sure that she got some more. It could have been a sort of pleasurable pain, but who am I to tell? It was however one home run after the other! The thrusts, that is.

She was in control while it lasted. She opened her floodgates and let the dam break down as she burst all over him. This happened a couple of times before she dismounted. She did not however exactly dismount. They simply rolled over to get him to the top without letting his manhood slip out of her. It was not an easy maneuver. She was however able to execute it with relative ease.

With both legs now kicking wildly into the air at nothing in particular he thrust and thrust again. The ecstasy was at its wildest and they were both soon to run out of breath. They were already sweating heavily when they began to slow down. It did not last too long for they had each achieved a series of volcanic eruptions, with each as uncontrollable as the next. With that series of fiery eruptions, rapture had been achieved as they had exploded into each other over and over again.

As soon as it was all over they fell on each other. They lay there on the floor like a pair of useless rags that were of no further use. They had been completely drained of energy, weakened and exhausted. They slept off like tired babies for this had become a routine with them. It had become their habit.

That evening they sat down together on the big oak table in their study. They now used it together with each person having a chair on either side. The table was big enough to accommodate both of them. He attended to his work and she to hers. They discussed whatever problems they had with their work together. It was a perfect union.

Late in the afternoon they opted for lunch in a restaurant in the town. It was their favorite seafood joint. They were ushered to a special table by the head chef who knew Johnny on a first name basis. He had heard of Joy but that was his first time of seeing her at close quarters. He did not fail to notice that she was quite a dish as had been rumored.

For this lunch they started off with tossed fruit salad. It contained amongst others: Olives, seedless grapes, peaches, nectarines, tangerines, pawpaw and avocado pears. The sweetener used with this was wild clove honey. After the salad came a dish that consisted of grilled salmon, sushi, lobster tails and young squid. For desert, it was non-fat Greek-style Yogurt, and for him there were a few raw oysters in lemon. Only the chef thought of the significance of this last addition.

It was not just the food that took him there, it was the vista. The restaurant was on the fifth floor of a commercial building. By the windows were small telescopic binoculars with which those eating could view the sea. Their special table was placed against one such window and so they could both eat and view at once. From there they could view the traveler's archipelago as well as fishermen at work. Various birds, especially sea gulls could be seen chasing the fishing trawlers. They were after the entrails of the fish as the fishermen gutted some of their catches.

From the restaurant they left for the museum. It was the museum of natural history which housed remains and reconstructions of animals past and present, especially the prehistoric ones. They started from the beginning when there were mainly dinosaurs. Joy was however more interested in the section that dealt with some of the old volcanic islands and the animals that dwelt there. The islands were not identified, but they contained remains and reconstructions of animals in various stages of evolutionary development. Some actually had both modern and prehistoric characteristics. One of them was a fish that had both well—developed lungs as well as gills.

They touched a few other places of interest before heading for the film theater. The film of the day was on its own. It was a sort of documentary, but it was full of rib-cracking humorous scenes. It was a film on individuals who had failed so abysmally in their fields of endeavor that they were now each regarded as champions. In other words it was a film that was dedicated to and in praise of failure. Its title was actually: "IN PRAISE OF FAILURE."

The very first episode was dedicated to a medical doctor. He was the head of the surgical unit of a teaching hospital. He was rumored to be very inept in his practice of the profession, but being the head of the department none dared air that view publicly. The film was on his unexpected activities as he performed surgery on his own mother.

His mother had left kidney failure and by a stroke of luck they had locked in on a donor. They were both prepared for the surgery and from there he took over. The surgery was over in record time and his mother was properly and promptly sown up. Within three days she had once more become a perfect candidate for dialysis. What was the problem? He had cut off her right kidney which was good and mistakenly once more replaced it with a bad one cut off from the patient before her. The donor was alright. She only lost one kidney which had been mistakenly discarded for bad.

The poor old lady had graduated from one bad kidney to two bad ones. To make matters worse, he had forgotten his pair of gloves in her stomach. It was an x-ray that made them realize that he had discarded the gloves in her stomach while also abandoning a pair of forceps there. It was reported as a simple case of 'lost and found'. She had to undergo a second operation for them to recover what they had lost.

The institution did not take any actions against him. Their official report was to the effect that it was family matter and so should be left private.

The next episode was a little bit more complicated though simpler. They were not very sure of what category to put it in. It was all about a master printer. He printed virtually all the official government documents for them and he was respected as well as trusted. It was not until the Bible society gave him a contract that the unimaginable happened. They wanted bibles to sell at a reduced rate to donors for money to use in poorer countries. They were also going to use them to spread the Word or Good news to all the four corners of the earth, as they had put it.

He did a very good job of it. But then came a miracle! They were not surprised since the bible was full of various miracles. Copies of that very edition were being snatched up everywhere and he had to print more. It took six months and four reprints before they discovered why the sales were so hot: There was a printing error in Exodus 20 Verse 14. He had unintentionally missed out the word "not" from that short verse. It therefore turned out to read: "Thou shalt commit adultery."

It was for this reason and for this reason only, that this edition had become a rare collection. Everyone was itching and eager to obey the word of God. He had generated a lot of money for the bible society and they never complained about that. They only asked him to put in for a recall of that edition, or preferably just publish an erratum.

Unfortunately, though expectedly, no one returned his. Not even the pastor who was known to have bought one agreed to return his own. One reverend father had insisted that it was justification for all he had done and so he refused to return his own. He intended to use it as evidence during the last judgment.

Then came the case of the popular and mathematically oriented servant. His master had sent him to the bank to cash a check for five hundred dollars for him. The man left for work and the boy parked his few belongings and headed for the bank. He was going to be a rich man and he intended to get lost from there.

All he did was to add a couple of harmless zeroes to the end of the amount on the check. His master had forgotten to put in the words and he intended to clean him out. He therefore helped him to fill out the words and he was ready to become rich. He went to the bank to cash his five million dollars check! First of all his master had only six hundred dollars in his name. More importantly however was the fact that only a madman could come to cash such an amount. He had actually come with two sacks and a wheelbarrow to wheel away his riches.

One thing led to another and in the end, the wardens in a correctional facility helped him store his belongings while he served his time. The judge found him so stupid that he sentenced him to five years in prison. It was however with the option of parole within six months. The condition for the parole was that he had to desist from any further mathematical maneuvers. The film did not go further to show what happened after that.

The next was about a preacher. He was the Right Reverend Jonathan Job. He had just been posted to one of those mega churches with over five thousand adherents coming in every Sunday.

He was such a great preacher that the congregants loved him. He always gave them a delightfully dull but never boring sermon. His sermons were always very dull but surprisingly, they were never boring. How could that be? The congregants always woke up very refreshed.

His voice had a sort of hypnotic effect on them. It always took just a few minutes from the beginning of his sermons for most of them to fall asleep. As one eye witness put it: "His voice was often like a soothing but cacophonic choir in the church." To make matters worse, people snored with reckless abandon to add substance to his voice. It was from every corner and they usually took off while he was still on the introductory phase of the sermons.

Listening to him was like being exposed to a perpetual lullaby. No one ever came out of it aware of what he had talked about and these sermons often lasted for well over two hours. Some were even convinced that not even he knew what he was preaching about. All they were sure of is that once he started heading for the preaching podium, they knew that it was time for siesta and it was always welcome. Only one man had ever lasted the entire sermon awake and he did so on a bottle of energy drink supported with a mug of strong black coffee.

He was once so eloquent in this his endeavor that he finished and left the church while the entire congregation was still fast asleep. He could have failed in bringing them closer to the Lord, but he had always managed to get them well rested, and that was the greatest introduction to modern ways of worship.

This preacher however had resounding ineptitude in a few other areas. On the day that he left the church without his adherents being aware of the fact that he was gone, it all happened because he was in a hurry to go and pick up his wife from the train station. She was to arrive on pier seven of the Huntington train station by three in the morning.

He dashed off from the church and took off for the Hutchinson train station. He was there till six in the evening without seeing anyone there. No train had arrived there and there was no one to ask. He was frustrated at the end and so went home without her. It was only after he made a call on the road that he found out what had happened.

In the first place, he was at the Hutchinson station instead of the Huntington station. One was on the eastern side of the city and the other on the western side. To make matters worse, there was only one reason why he did not see anyone there. That particular station had been closed for well over six months. Furthermore, he was to pick up his wife by three in the morning, but he had passed the night in his girlfriend's house and went there by three in the evening instead. In other words, he was twelve hours late!

This was followed by the escapades of a thief who had broken most of the major rules of burglary. He had stealthily stolen into a bank during working hours and hid in one of the closets there. After closing hours he decided to take his time and rob the bank. The place was well lit and so he decided to turn off some of the lights.

The very first switch that he turned off happened to be a panic button. He had actually turned it on, or rather triggered it off. It immediately alerted the police from their station. The police were there in no time and he panicked. He simply ran into the manager's restroom and hid in the tub there. It turned out to be the tub which the painter had used to mix some of the paints that he used that afternoon to repaint part of the bank. As soon as he realized that he had just dived into a tub of paint he jumped out and decided to clean it off with some universal solvent that he saw nearby. What he just poured on himself turned out to be sulfuric acid.

As soon as he realized that it was an acid and that it might eat into his clothes and skin, he cried out to the police for help. That was how they found out where he was. In one simple masterstroke, he had literarily arrested himself.

It was this same burglar that had once slept off in the middle of a burglary. He had slept off and snored so loudly that the people he came to rob awoke and arrested him in his sleep. He was having headache and so he took some pills from their medicine cabinet for it. It was unfortunately sleeping pill and it acted fast. He managed to slip off from them, but it was only to find out that all the doors had been locked and so he decided to escape through the chimney. He got stuck there and so used his cell phone to call the emergency department for help. The fire brigade and police arrived at the same time to extricate him from there and arrest him. Once more he had played a major part in his own arrest. In this particular case it turned out that he had been arrested twice for the same offence as it were.

There were a couple of other episodes before the film ended. It was a very entertaining film and one could tell that from how people roared in laughter. As for Johnny, he already had a mild headache from the laughter by the time it all ended.

It was Johnny that drove the car on their way home. Funny enough, though expectedly, the headache vanished as soon as they got home. It was Joy that cured him.

She had started undressing very close to him. The sight of her undressing was enough to make him relegate the headache to the background. Love was in the air. He was already rigid and stiff like a magician's wand. His phallus was also beginning to drip like saliva from a furious rodeo bull.

By the time he got close to her, she was already breathing irregularly. They were shallow breaths that arose from anticipation. She purposely turned to hang her cloth in the closet, but he was already on her. He hugged her from the back and she flinched while arching her entire body backwards. She had surrendered backwards to him and right into his arms. She knew what he was capable of doing.

He did not waste time before he started to knead her nipples and he stroked them in every given direction. He was gentle with that. She felt the warmth of his action and her nipples began to stiffen and then harden into hard protuberances. She moaned. It was that type of happy contented moan as she surrendered herself to him even more. Her eyes were now fully shot as she savored those heavenly touches.

He then suddenly dropped one of his hands to where one could consider as her center of gravity. As soon as his fingers traced a path through that area she went wild with ecstasy. She muttered all sorts of sweet nothings, some meaningless, some unintelligible and many in tongues unknown to either of them. He was certain that she had just acquired that ability to speak in tongues. Maybe she learnt it from the Bishop.

She had had enough! She suddenly wheeled around and with shaking hands went for his manhood. She attempted to roll them in her palm, but she was actually sizing it up, trying to remember what size it was. Without any further ado and fanfare, she thrust it right into her yearning womanhood.

She had thrust it in with such reckless abandon that she almost felt the pain of that forceful penetration. He did not help matters either since he was now also at the peak of his own excitement. It was a sudden and unannounced entrance into that her chamber of warmth and it essentially knocked him off his senses.. He was now carrying her with her legs firmly wrapped around his waist.

As they gyrated and banged against each other his phallus slid out, but he quickly reinserted it. He did so this time around with a little more care and respect. It was at this point of reentry that his organ began to inject its load of fluid into her.

She was eager and ready for him. She held tighter, but this time around, she was holding his buttocks while trying to push it as much as possible closer to her, and if possible into her. He did not disappoint her for she did not want him to waste any of that precious fluid. She wanted it all inside her and she wanted it all as far inside as possible. He did not waste time before letting her derriere perch on the side of the table as they banged so ferociously against each other that the table almost lost one of its legs.

Sweat cascaded down their entire bodies as they once more climaxed at one and the same time. They were each completely worn out by the time this was over and each of them was desperately gasping for precious air. How they managed to fall to the floor had remained a miracle. They were both on the floor while hanging on dearly to each other. They slept off in each other's arms till nightfall.

That was how the cash family spent that weekend. It was in anticipation of the coming week. It was going to be a grueling work week. He was going to be out of the country for three days to negotiate for buyers for their new products. Joy was also going to be off for about two days to a nearby developing country to recruit cheap labor for the company. This country had always been a source of cheap labor for any company that wanted them.

Johnny and joy had been together in this conjugal union for about a year now. Passion between them was still as hot as it was when they came together, if not more. Things were however probably going to take a negative turn.

Johnny was the most popular chief executive officer that the company had ever seen, but Joy was beginning to soar in popularity too. She did not have to ask for anything before getting it. Johnny was not worried about her. He trusted her and he knew that she could always stand her own. He however knew that some men were wolves and some were foxes, and that worried him a little bit. She might come across some of these two groups once in a while and he was not too sure of how she was going to resist them. On her own part, she knew that he was very popular and particularly so with the women. She was a woman and she was afraid that he might fall to their advances one of these days.

She had gossiped with them before, and she knew what they thought of him. She had always trusted him, but nowadays it has come with a little reservation. The stage was therefore now set for possible unhitching, going by her language.

On Monday morning, Johnny left for his trip abroad. He left in his private jet with a pilot, a copilot as well as his secretary. Halima was her name. She, Halima, was a complete knock out by her own standards, just like Joy. She was pretty, but it was in her own way. She was a cutie in every sense of the word and quite sociable. Unlike Joy however, that natural magnetism was not there. It might be very unfair to compare the two of them. The only way to put it is that if she was a stunner, then Joy was a killer, when it came to beauty. Helen of Troy would have been very jealous of Joy.

Before Joy came into his life, Johnny was not interested in women except for occasional flings. Halima was pretty and they were always cooped together and just for that reason there was that rumor that they were dating each other. This was however totally unfounded. He made sure that he had nothing to do with anyone that worked for the company. The workers did not feel that nothing was going on. They believed that something was cooking between the two. It was just a rumor and a false one at that. That rumor happened to filter its way, mistakenly or as planned, into Joy's ears. She was careful not to let him know that she heard such a rumor. She had not forgotten what he said when she told him that she was into the escort business.

They had just met and taken to each other. She felt that if she did not tell him of her darker secrets whenever he found out he would not take kindly to it. It was therefore better to reveal it right at the beginning. She was pleasantly surprised as well as delighted when he said: "let bygones be bygones."

She therefore applied the same principle in this case, but that was if it was true.

She had met Halima in his office a couple of times and she had also come to their house to drop off documents for him. She was a very polite girl. Joy did not however fail to notice that she was beautiful as well as fairly much younger than she was. That kept her on the edge and she had also become a little bit apprehensive towards the poor girl. She even went as far as to asking Johnny to sack her when she made a minor mistake.

On that faithful morning Halima came to their house to pick up the paper work that they would need during the tour. She was the secretary to the Chief Executive Officer of the company and so she dressed in a way that would be befitting of that post. That was one of the reasons that tongues wagged. They felt that she dressed so well just to trap Johnny. Some of them even claimed that she could not afford some of the dresses that she wore. The insinuation was that her boss bought them for her. They were all lies anyway. She earned more than most of them and she had no family ties.

Halima's parents had died when she was still a child and according to the records, she was less than a year old when they both died in a fatal motor accident. The authorities tried to trace her relatives but it was to no avail. She therefore grew up at the mercy of some reverend sisters in a convent. Those who knew her in school were still surprised that, based on her behavior; she did not go in for the priesthood.

It was most probably petty jealousy or maybe simple envy that led to all those rumors. Each of them would have loved to be in her shoes, though for different reasons. In fact, the very person who had started off those rumors happened to be her best friend Candace. Candace was the unofficial mouthpiece or itinerant radio without battery for the establishment. She was in charge of all the unofficial information around. A few were true, but most of them were false and simply products of the figments of her extremely fertile imagination.

Anyway, Joy was not her usual self when Halima came in to their house that morning. She felt that the young girl was too well dressed and too pretty to be going all about with her husband. They were going to spend three to four days cooped together and jetting all around the world. She did not however dare to voice her concerns. This was not just because there might be nothing to it, but also because she had her own cross to bear. In fact she knew Candace all too well and so she was surprised that she even thought that way at all. She had heard that Candace herself was once interested in her husband, but he had turned her down.

With Johnny, it was just about the same story and concern about Joy. Joy would be leaving the following day with one of her assistants—the deputy director of social services. That was Tommy Boy. No one knew how he came by that name, but it was the only name that he had. He was a patented philanderer but that did not seem to affect his work. He was still unattached and a fairly handsome young man. To complicate matters, he was a lady's man. He was one of those that could be said to have that ability to talk a hungry monkey down from a fruit tree that was laden with fruit. In other words his tongue could convince any woman to get into bed with him.

Some had it that he had already gone to bed with every lady there, married or single. Anything in skirts was fair game. Johnny believed that it was an exaggeration. He was twenty six and he had joined them at twenty four. Before then, he had just been terminated from his previous job. Though he was a very smart and intelligent character, it was his activities with members of the opposite sex that got him into trouble. In high school, he was two classes ahead of his age mates. He was however known to have slept with their mathematics teacher. She was incidentally about five years older than his mother.

In university, he put away the five year course in two and a half years. At the tender age of twenty one he had earned his doctorate degree. While still in his undergraduate section, he had managed to get the wife to their dean pregnant. This resulted in a big scandal. The dean was about to retire early and he was also known to be impotent. He had made a "cougar" out of the Dean's wife. She was the departmental Librarian, the post that she had held for at least seventeen years. They met each other very often between the rows of books in the library. At times they used the table in the stock room.

The dean did not mind. At least he now had a son. Tommy had become the laughing stock of the entire school but that did not border him. What he lacked in character, he made up for in the academics.

As soon as he graduated, he was snapped up by the space agency. He worked as a go-between, between their astronauts and those from other countries. He was quartered at the head office of the space agency. No sooner than one of these space men left for a four month duty in the international space station than his wife got pregnant. It was obvious that the pregnancy was not from the space man. His wife was about the same age with Tommy's grandmother but it did not matter to him.

It was not until they went for a paternity test that it was discovered that Tommy Boy had done it again. It was when it was confirmed that he was the father of the child that his appointment was terminated. He was terminated on the grounds of inappropriate sexual behavior as was contained in the company's handbook. Johnny knew all this before hiring him. He was a very efficient worker none the less.

There was that saying that "a leopard can never change its spots." His character had remained with him, Tommy Boy that is. Johnny was a little bit concerned but he was also aware of the fact that Joy could hold her own no matter the condition. What he did not put into consideration was the fact that Joy herself was probably not going to change who she was too. Both Tommy Boy and Joy had been mandated with going to the nearby country to hire cheap labor. It was the brain child of Joy. It would save them a lot of money, but more importantly they would fall into the good books of the government. They wanted to have a closer tie with that country. The country had a lot of uranium deposits and they were interested in that.

Johnny was very happy with Joy for that. It was her brain child. As soon as it was known that two of them were going to travel together, tongues began to wag. They tried to map out what was going to happen when these two were unleashed against each other in a foreign country without anyone to watch over them. They were sure that Tommy boy would live to expectation, but Johnny did not think so.

While Johnny took off in his private jet with Halima, Joy left in a charter plane in the opposite direction with Tommy Boy. This was going to usher in the beginning of the end of their marital bliss. Johnny had chased Joy all over as the wind and he had succeeded in bottling this wind. Right now the chances were that the bottled wind might get unbottled.

Both Johnny and Joy returned from their trips the same day. It was just as if they had planned it. Their planes arrived at the airport at the same time and so Johnny was asked to circle the area a few times to let Joy land. As Johnny circled the airport his friends at the control tower told him that they were waiting for Joy to land before him.

As for Joy, she was not expecting him till the following day. Johnny had finished his mission a day early and so he headed home. Joy was very much at ease when they arrived and so she went on in a nonchalant manner. Johnny's plane finally landed and as they slowly moved past the back entrance to their parking spot, they saw Joy going out.

She was heading for the exit with nothing in hand except Tommy Boy's attaché case. Tommy Boy followed behind luging the remaining three suit cases. One was the small light one that belonged to him, but the other two heavy ones belonged to Joy. She had bought a lot of presents over there for her friends and coworkers. She also had two tote bags but Tommy Boy had them slung over his shoulders, one on either side.

To Johnny, that was a queer arrangement. A certain degree of familiarity must be there for him to agree to labor under the weight of all her things. It is not that he can't help her with her load, but it did not have to be all of them as he did. It did not however ring any bell and so he simply let it be. It was just one of those things.

For the mean time two Limousines had been sent over to pick them up from the airport. One was to pick up Joy and the other Tommy Boy, but they managed to ride in the same one. Johnny eventually went home in the abandoned Limo.

Rumors were already flying about when they came back to work. In the entourage that went with Joy were two other ladies. The idea was to show case them. They were hiring for equivalent positions and she wanted people to see them. It was going to be a great incentive and it worked. Many people wanted to be like them. For these poor applicants, to be like those women was like heading for heaven. They never negotiated for their salaries. They were each offered something way below twenty percent of what these women earned.

Joy and Tommy Boy had checked into the Hotel Excelsior while those other two women were checked into the Hotel Sofitel. They were therefore some five miles away from each other. The people at home felt that it was a deliberate arrangement to give them some privacy. They were however not sure of what went on there or what did not go on.

Johnny's closest confidant in the whole place was not Halima as one would expect. It was the old janitor that cleaned his office. She was rumored to be about ninety years old and she always called Johnny her son. She was the first person to talk when they chanced on each other in the office early in the morning:

"Welcome back sir." She greeted.

"Thanks Ruth. How have you been?"

"I've been alright. There was nothing to do since you were not there to dirty the place."

"I suspected so. At least you are well rested now." He said this with a chuckle.

"Of course I am well rested, and how was the trip?"

"Very successful."

"Very good. That means that we might soon be bracing for a raise."

"Who said that?"

"I guessed that if you did well then more money will come in. I guess that it will trickle down to us at the end."

"I hope you are not campaigning for a raise."

"How can. I was just pulling your legs."

"Why can't you?"

"Because I know what others earn in other companies as well as what a lot of people earn here. I know that I earn more than most of my peers here too."

"I thought that wages were secret for each individual so how did you know?"

"Walls have ears you know."

"I agree with you."

"Sir, I hope you know that I treat you as my son?"

"I know that."

"Is there any other thing that you want me to do?"

"No, but what is the problem?"

"What problem?"

"I know that there is something that is worrying you."

"Me? No."

"Ruth!"

"Yes sir."

"Tell me what is bordering you. I hope you know that I can read you like a book."

"Promise not to get annoyed with me when I tell you what it is."

"Have I ever been annoyed with you before?"

"No. It is something personal though I don't believe it."

"Believe what?"

"The rumors that have been going around."

"What rumors?"

"By the way, I haven't seen Halima today. She usually comes in very early."

"She went for emergency office supplies."

"About time too. Two days ago there were no memo pads left."

"Why are you changing the topic?"

"I am not."

"Then it is about Halima that you want to tell me."

"Yes and no."

"Yes and no?"

"Yes because it is about her and no because it isn't exactly about her."

"Since when have you become a lawyer?"

"Why a lawyer?"

"They usually talk from either side of their mouths at once."

"Well it is about her, but it is also about you."

"That makes sense; after all she is my secretary."

"Not that."

"Then what?"

"They claim that you have been dating her." Johnny immediately went livid with anger but he tried not to take it out on her.

"Where did those rumors come from?"

"No idea. I only heard it from one of the girls."

"How dare they think of that, not to talk of saying it? Let me just get my hands on the person who started it. I made and know the rules so why should it be me who will break them? First of all, if I dated her we are likely to get so cozy that it will affect our duties. Secondly it is against company policy to do that between coworkers and they are not even allowed to buy gifts over a certain amount for each other. Finally the punishment for trying that is termination of appointment. How then do you think that I will try that?"

"Sir, I know that it is a lie. They must have started it out of jealousy."

"They never said that when I was single so why now that I am married?"

"Now that you asked that question, something else just crossed my mind."

"What is that?"

"Let me keep it with me for now."

"Not even to your son?'

"No, not even to you."

"Okay, you know best."

"I think I should be going."

"Thanks Ruth. I am glad that you told me what had been going on."

Johnny was worried by what he heard. He had never taken too kindly to false accusations. If his wife got wind of these false rumors, only God knows where it will lead to. That night he found it hard to sleep, but he made sure that Joy did not suspect that he was restless or worried. He suddenly remembered everything and went sullen. Joy noticed that. He instead blamed it all on jet lag and overexertion. When Ruth came in the following morning, he sat her down for a thorough interrogation.

"Sit down Ruth." He had ordered as she came in with her broom. It was the first time that he had ever asked her to sit down and so she knew that something serious was in the air.

"Where should I sit?" She asked.

"Sit on that sofa by the side."

Ruth felt very uneasy and nervous as she sat down. She was already regretting having told him about what she heard.

"As you were leaving yesterday, you said something to the effect that you had a hunch?" Johnny asked.

"Yes Sir."

"What was it?"

"I would have preferred to keep it to myself."

"I could not sleep last night and so you just have to tell me."

"Sir the reason why I did not want to tell you is that they are mere suspicions. Why not let me confirm them before telling you, otherwise I would be like all those gossipers."

"Two heads are always better than one. Let's put our minds together and the mystery will be solved." She hung her head low, looking on the floor and thinking for a few minutes before she replied:

"Sir, I also heard a couple of other rumors yesterday that made me think that I might be right about my hunches."

"What are the other rumors?"

"They claimed that during the tour, Joy and Tommy Boy checked into one Hotel and sent the other two off to another."

"And what is wrong with that? Senior executives and junior officers usually don't check into the same hotel."

"That's not the problem."

"What's the problem then?"

"It was alleged that they both checked into the same room."

"How did they know that?"

"Do you remember Bianca?"

"Yes. What about her?"

"She is from there."

"And so what?"

"The attendant who served them for those three days in the hotel happens to be Bianca's cousin."

With that, Johnny stood up and paced the room for a few minutes. Ruth simply kept quiet because it was obvious that he was deeply in thought. He then suddenly came to Joy's defense though he was not too sure of why he had to do that:

"Supposing they stayed in the same room during the day and in the early hours of the night due to the pressure of work and then separated when it was time to go to bed. Don't you think that was the situation?"

"Her cousin insisted that they paid for only one room."

"That could be easily verified."

"How?"

"When they retire their imprest account we will see the receipts."

"They can always arrange for extra receipts. Anyway I can see that you trust your wife a lot."

"Yes I do, and I love her."

"No wonder they say that love is blind."

"In what way?"

"It will not let you see through her."

"And what have you seen yourself?"

"Just what I told you."

"And you believe it?"

"Initially I did not, but now I know it to be true."

"And what made you change your mind?"

"I have known you for many years and I know that you did not do any of those things that they said you did. In the case of your wife don't forget that I am a woman and so I can read through her. You may not understand our ways. I do not know much about her past, but as a woman, I know that she must have seen the world and must have enjoyed the finer things of life before. She must have also enjoyed life itself to the fullest, with no holds barred if you know what I mean. To me, she is like a tamed lion. Tame it as you may, it will always remain a wild animal at heart. She had been around, if I may put it that way, and she can always revisit her past."

Johnny listened to her silently, pondered on every word she said and he seemed to make some sense out of what she said.

"What you are saying is that if she used to be bad, then she had just gone back to being bad."

"If you put it that way, yes."

"Please promise me that you will never tell anyone what I am about to tell you now."

"I promise."

"Before we met, she was a call girl."

"God forbid! And you still went ahead and married her?"

"To me the past was the past. What mattered was the present and the future."

"As for the present you might be correct, but when it comes to the future, don't try to second guess what it will hold in store."

"In what way?"

"Trust me. The only thing that she thinks of about the future is likely to be her freedom. Believe me; I have seen that in her. I did not know anything about her before I started telling you about my hunches. Please rely on my wisdom."

"I will." He looked very sullen. He looked down on the floor in deep thought for a few minutes. It was only then that he was able to say what he had believed about her:

"I believed that with me around, she will not want anything else."

"Can you know and do you know what a woman wants?"

"I am no longer sure."

"I don't either. No one knows what a woman wants, not even the woman herself. At times what a woman will want will defy all logical explanations."

"What exactly are you saying?"

"That she might be thinking of changing over to Tommy Boy."

"If that's what she wants then I'll wish her all the luck."

"Right now, I am sure that she does not suspect that you know anything about them."

"I am sure of that."

"If I know women very well, I believe that she triggered off that rumor about you and Halima."

"Why would she do that?"

"To provide grounds for a divorce."

"But if she wants a divorce all she has to do is to ask for it."

"But that might not be lucrative enough. If she files on the grounds that you are seeing another woman, then she gets over fifty percent of what you own."

"You make a lot of sense, but I will try to find out."

"How?"

"I'll try to set a trap for her or rather for them. Please thank you."

"You are welcome."

It was only then that Johnny began to see things like other people. His mind went back to when he saw them at the airport and everything was beginning to make sense now. He was going to set a trap for them, by pretending to travel out for two days. He knew that Tommy Boy had a soft spot for Hotel Excelsior just outside the city. He told Joy and all that he was jetting off for two days. Instead he checked into that hotel.

To Joy, he was going off on an international meeting for two days. Nothing was going to go wrong at home since they now had a house maid. He was sure that the trap would catch them. The manager of the hotel used to be his private driver before he secured that job for him. That was how he knew of all of Tommy's trysts there.

He had arranged with the manager for a hidden camera in one of their best rooms. This happened to be the room that Tommy always asked for. The camera was triggered off by motion and there were two monitors, one in the mangers office and the other in the room that was given to him. It was the adjoining room.

He left that afternoon for the hotel, while his pilot took off to a neighboring airport. Tommy's favorite room was room six hundred and six. He was in room six hundred and four just next to them. By seven thirty in the evening Tommy Boy checked in. A few minutes later Joy followed. Tommy had called to inform her that the coast was clear and that was when she came in. He watched as she went in, closed the door and then ran into his arms. They smooched as if they had not seen each other in a while. It was only after that introductory act that they began to talk. It was Tommy that started it off:

"Hello Honeybun, how I wish he takes off like this more often."

"I feel the same way too."

"I hope he wouldn't ever get suspicious."

"Johnny? No way. He is so much in love and trusts me so much that even if he caught us in the act he still wouldn't believe that anything was going on." They laughed over that as he watched, but he did not find it funny.

"I hope you know that I might even trust you more than that?"

"I already know that sweetheart."

"Do you know that way back in Oceania, I would never have imagined that you would ever consider getting together with me."

"But from the first time I set eyes on you, I have been having all sorts of fantasies about you."

"But why didn't I know. See how I have wasted an entire year of bliss."

"That's no problem. We can always make up for it."

"When exactly is he coming back?"

"Day after tomorrow. In the evening."

"In that case would you like me to remain here for three days?"

"That would be lovely."

"I hope you have not forgotten that I had asked you to marry me?'

"But I did give you an answer."

"No."

"Sure, I did."

"You only said that one had to get unhitched first before getting re-hitched."

"Exactly."

"But that is neither yes nor no."

"I hope you know that a woman cannot have more than one husband at a time?"

"I know that."

"And that's why I have to get unhitched first."

"What of if it fails?"

"It will not fail. Don't forget that I have already set him up."

"Are you sure that the plan will work?"

"I am very sure, and it will come with quite some money too for us."

"What sort of money are you talking about?"

"Johnny is worth well over nine hundred million and at least half of it will come my way. With that sort of money we can go places sweetie."

"Oh my sweetheart, that's why I love you so much."

"The court might even throw the jet into the bargain. That jet actually belongs to him and the company only leases it from him for his own use."

"That's a fraudulent arrangement."

"Not exactly. They needed a jet for company use and they did not have the money and so he bought it for himself. The company was too embarrassed and so they offered to pay whenever he was using it for company business. That made it cheaper for them."

"It is rumored that the plane is even more advanced than the presidential plane."

"It is."

"How did he manage to get so rich?" He asked next.

"He was actually the inventor of the new series of microchips that everyone manufactures nowadays, and he holds patent rights to it. For that reason, any company that manufactures it pays some royalty to him."

"Now I get the picture. Are you hungry?"

"No. Just something to drink."

Johnny watched on as he ordered a bottle of champagne that was delivered in record time. As the drink was being brought in, she vanished into the toilet only to reappear when the person who brought it in left. She did not want to take any chances at being seen. He sat on the sofa, and she on his laps as they sipped their drink. Johnny had seen it all first hand.

It might not be out of place here to point to how Johnny felt. He was deeply in love with Joy and he saw her slipping away from him. She was now going with another person which gave rise to the impression that she had sort of abandoned him and refused his advances. He called it the apparent debacle of love. It was on how he felt about her in the moment of confusion in his mind.

For one to watch his wife with another man was definitely very painful, but to hear them plot against him at the same time was something else. He was deeply in love with her and he was totally committed to the marriage, but there she was on her devious way out of the marriage.

As he spent his idle time in the room penning down his mind, he was not too sure of whether it was what he felt at that very moment or what he could have felt had she abandoned him much earlier. Maybe he would have felt so if she had left him for another man, be that before or now, it did not matter:

The Apparent Debacle Of Love

Like a solitary rose in a bush of thorns
So you stand out among the rest—
Oh my love, you will never fade.
In bed at night I've longed for you
When I toss and pine for you.
But to find you I never could
Since your heart is in a secret place
From where I could never decipher it.
Though tied to and caged with another soul
Your smile still intoxicates my afflicted soul,
With a laugh that's even more hypnotic.
I see you as a thief, for all I know
For you have stolen my pounding heart.
When I sleep that waking sleep at night—
When my eyes sleep but my mind keeps awake—
My head is always filled with you.

My soul did wait in high expectations—
Expectations doomed to be unfulfilled.
Though I could never experience your love
I'll always think of you.
For my soul dearly longs for you
And my body crazily thirsts for you
Like the desert in thirst for rain;
For your love to me is sweeter than life itself;
Though I seem to think it's all in vain.

Within arm's length and yet further than far,
Attainable and yet unattainable.
Like a shadow you seem to come to me
While my soul follows hard after you.
When I approach and come close to you
You always fade into nothing but you—
Nothing that could douse my fiery wants.
It's often then and only then
That those tumultuous billows arise
And then into my imagination arrive
To taunt my sea of hopeless hope
Into desolation without any hope
And cast me away for to be forever forgotten by you,
Though you elude my tottering goals
You are etched forever into my tormented soul.
My eyes are not satisfied to just see you,
Neither my ears just to your soothing voice
With each consumed by that desire for you and you
    alone.
My heart had looked for you and none but you
Unable to seek for only you
For madness and folly had taken their toll on me
As fear of rejection grips my heart
In pangs of throbbing and piercing pains
Grief had compounded itself with sorrow that pants
To heed your innocent and subtle wants.
Though you seem to love me too
Those constraints seem to hurt and hurt us both.

Consumed by that fire of love for you,
Drowned in that sea of desire and want
I eagerly await a tryst with you;
Though sore and weary from that noble creed.
I descend fast and faster indeed
Into the depths of desires unfulfilled.
My spirit remains overwhelmed and troubled—
So troubled I no longer think with ease
As turbulence and grief invade my soul.

I had delighted in the thoughts of you,
I had delighted in being with you;
But a shadow can never be with one.
Though my heart is forever yours and yours alone
Not minding the fact that it should have with another
been
My desires had come to no avail.
WHEN FULFILLED YOU MIGHT HURT LIKE ME
AND IF UNFULFILLED I MIGHT HURT SOME
    MORE.
EVEN IF UNFULFILLED I MIGHT HURT LIKE YOU
FOR YOUR HURT WILL HURT ME OH MY LOVE
AND THAT IS THE STRANGE DEBACLE OF
    LOVE—

Total uncommitted love—
That very love that I have for you.
Like a man on a fool's errand
In search of Ulysses Gold in the veldt
That was never to be found and held,
I strive to fulfill my love for you.
What a fool I have been
For folly had made me its hiding place.
Distance yourself from that lovely piece
And give your soul a chance for peace;
But then,
It seems easier said than done.

I mourn this loss of my lovely love
And life will never be the same again
For unfulfilled expectations have marked my lot.
Thunder strikes but once they say
But twice it has struck on me
I regret
I mourn
I wail
I cry
And I weep oh my love—
For I am drowning in that sea of elusive love.

With delight my heart skips at the sight of you.
It always skips with joy.
But your fire has consumed my innermost heart
Letting it just into the twilight of love—
That twilight of loving love.
Diligently I have looked for you
And yet I find you not,
Solace in your arms had been my hope
But it whittles as I look some more
Yet meekly I seek and follow your love.
Oft disappointed and abandoned with a broken heart
I have been led into a narrow and deep ditch
And it's hard to retrace her slippery walls.

Please set not your eyes on me again
For that would more crazy make me now.
Those malicious and cruel effects
From your reasonable and innocent goals
Have pummeled and pulverized my ailing soul
Into that state of abject misery.
With thoughts of unimaginable dejection
And those of seeming rejection
I had wined to ease my hurt with ease, but it failed to
aid my misery.
I had opened my heart to my lovely love
I had approached your enchanted being
But your gateman had locked me out.

Once I nearly saw your tears
And they looked like early lovely morning drops
Almost extracting the same from my confused eyes;
Yet your thoughts I could not decode.
But you are beautiful Oh my love
Though your heart is turned from me
And your decisions though true are terrible—
Terrible like a Tank division without any love—
Have hurt and hurt me bad,
Though it also hurts you too.
I am aware of the fact that you are good
And though in pains 'am delighted to see your face.
How pleasant I find you Oh my love
For you have stirred my innermost feelings—
You have awakened my innermost awakenings.
My love for you will never cease
As I'll forever love you and you alone.

Your love does no compassion spare
As it beams from far away
To slay my soul as it thinks and wills.
Oh how I wish for a taste of you
Though wishful thinking it all might be
For you have rather shunned my wants.
I searched, I groped and I looked for you
I wanted, I yearned and I craved for you
But only my unseeing eye could see you there
As I felt you with my unfeeling hands.

Oh how I love to be with you my love—
To love and cherish you with all my will.
Evasive those wants and desires do peer from you—
Wants that'll always be in vain.
Your love can make and unmake my soul
But it can happiness bring to it
Though sadness seems to be my fate and lot.
Oh wicked love! You harbinger of all my woes
How I fear your deadly grip on me
Yet your presence is love to me.
Being the one that I truly love.

Your mouth is full of kindness Oh my love
And wisdom oftener comes from it.
Not given to idle bouts in life
You have strived to beat the odds
And you should enjoy the fruits that come from it.
For strength and honor had marked your path.
Being bitterly enslaved to the thoughts of you
I'd neglected the chores assigned to me
For you skip and leap within my brain.

Innocent uttering had come from your lovely lips
Yet your ways remain unknown to me.
I did not obey those voices of constraint
Neither did I heed your warning signs
But blinded by pleasing love for you
I had failed to see the light.

I now languish in excruciating pain
As my soul in anguish aptly wilts.
Neither sleep nor slumber could find its way
Into my tired and weary eyes
Being chased away by that hunter of sleep.

I had inclined my ears to your lovely words
I had thought of all you said
I had cried my eyes sore and dry
To what it is I felt from you;
Though I feel you felt the same.
Straight and pleasing you seem to me
And happily I pine to be with you
But it's a quest to no avail—
A quest that's doomed to fail at last.
I was struck dumb and silent with sorrow
As your words stirred up endless horrors
That made my heart very hot within
And to burn with bitter and callous pain.
Though I'd have to nurse my wounded soul
For that's the only choice I have
I still will crave for you
And only the physician will have to heal himself.

I was immersed in sorrow so deep and great
That my eyes have cried themselves dry of tears.
My head had ached with a thousand aches
As that chamber of sorrows was unleashed on me.

Relative peace might eventually come to me—
Peace which sorrow might really be—
As sorrow that's only less sorrowful than sorrow
Since peace of mind might never come to me.

I was not deprived of you by you
I was not deprived of you by me
But circumstances and situations had both connived
And maneuvered to torture my tired soul.
I have however resolved to ever love you my love
And to tell you the truth no matter what.
Afflicted and wounded I've yet failed to hate your ways
But seem to be sure of this:
That I'll never come to taste your love again—
What a hideous lot for me.

With my eyes I have seen my love
And with my ears I've heard your loving voice.
With my hands I've reached for you my love
But you'll never come to be with me
For so it seems it's meant to be.

I can never speak an ill of you
With neither thoughts to hate your ways.
I can never flee from those thoughts of you
Though you have led me into that nook—
A hiding place carved for my weary soul—
The antechamber to my loneliness—

The loneliness of the presence of your absence
Loneliness so lonely
It's even lonelier than loneliness itself.
Loneliness born of apparent deprivation,
Deprivation from that unfulfilled love
From my one and only true love.

I know your love will forever be
But I'll try to reduce her grip on me.
I've tried to ease you out of my mind
But it had come to no avail.
For true love everlasting does remain.
I have tried to find some fault in you—
Fault to help me love you less,
But none had come for all I tried;
But had one ever even come
I would probably even loved you more
For though my soul tormented had been,
It still dotes on you and you alone.
My desires have attained their highest peak
For you've become an obsession for this restless soul;
But like that ephemeral shadow that you are
You have once more slipped from me
As hurt and dejected once more I am,
Steeped with love and hopeless pain.

It's not your fault that you deny me your love
For madness had blinded my inner thoughts.
There's only one option left for me
Having lived in denial of truth till now—
To retrace my steps anon.
I have to retreat as far as I could
Or else those pangs will increase the more
Through the times that will always come.
From you I have failed to run
Neither from me could I run.
True love is hard to leave behind
For love is really blind as they say
And often deals like a double-edged knife
That hurts any that comes its way.
Whether it be me or you.
Blinding love could well be cured
But who is that physician to do this job?
It is none other but me alone.
Physician please heal yourself!
That's if you could but uncover the ways of love.

Broken-hearted and unable to think
Wounded and in deep darkness I remain.
Please do show me the way
Please do tell me what to do anon
Please help quench this killer storm in me
Please help stop this tormenting of my soul
For I cannot be more broken-hearted than this,
Neither more dispirited either to get.

Please help restore the joy of life to me
And cast me not away from you
For you are the only one I truly love—
My only one and true love—
Though I know constraints remain.

Now I know I can never be with you
Neither can I fulfill my thirst for you.
It might be time for me to unthink my hopeless thoughts
Of loving and holding on to you
But then I can hardly let you go
For my love for you is from deep within
Etched in and never to erode away—
Everlasting love that has come to be
And though unfulfilled it its unable to leave.
Oh how I deeply love you Oh my love
For dazzled and in confusion still I do.

Love can make and unmake a man
It can make the heart to skip with joy
Just as it could also come as a lake of fire.
It could calm and succor bring to the soul
But only turmoil and pain it brings to me
Having tampered with the one there before.
Love could often self-destruct at will
The same love that could bring eternal peace
Or easily lead to war with ease.
I cannot predict what it wants from me
But for now it torments my miserable soul.

Though I still partake of your loving love.
I feel disemboweled on your slaughtering slab
Though I know you can nourish and becalm my soul
And probably tame my roving thoughts.
Oh how I yearn for a taste of you!
You apple of my craving heart,
You lovely angel that had stolen my heart—
Oh how I yearn to cherish and love your being!

Torment me not my dear love
For my lonely heart still craves for you.
Unleash your love on me
That I might finally have some peace in your arms.
Your love seems to have been carried by the wind
To fly further and further away from me
And despair had come to live with me,
As heavyhearted I mourn your loss.
Oh my love do come back to me
Do come back to me oh my love!

Though ordained to eternal bliss
Still in turbulence my heart dwells.
Maybe unworthy of your precious love
And persecuted by your unfulfilled love
I live in distress and yearn for you the more.
Let the wicked arm of your love stay her hand
For humbled, my heart now bows in despair.
I see those arrows come for me—

Those arrows of hurting love
As I recoil from the one I love
Though it's all to no avail.
The sorrow of your loss still haunts my heart
And yet I see those arrows come for me
And as a fierce army they come for my heart
To devour the entrails of this aching heart.

You are worthier than precious gem to me
And you have eluded me like one as well;
Abandoned to rot in my fruitless quest
My resolve is gone as you pierced through my heart
As desolate and afflicted, in distress I hurt,
And yet my desire for you leaps in bounds.
Oh for a taste of your blissful love!
To ease this sadness from my heart.
The voice of your love thunders through me
But its only her grieves that she rains on me.
By day and by night I think of you,
Troubled and in sorrow I await for you.
Why should love be so cruel to me?
I have waited in patience all for you,
Neither have I held my thoughts from you.
In anticipation my heart pounds for you
But unfulfilled in agony I languish too.
As that sword of unfulfillment tears through me
Diverse painful cries come from me
While I still await for you.

Oh my love, for how long will I wait for you?
As though cast away, I still await in vain,
For my soul still longs for you.
Though even a swallow could find a home with ease,
My lonely heart still homeless is.
It is void of those loving fruits of love—
Void though still awaiting you.

Please do not harden your heart against me
And do not withhold your love from me
For as the heat melts the wax with ease
So does your love melt the resolve in me.
I am helpless against your charm
So come to me Oh my love
That my heart might once again skip with joy
And come to love you with all my heart.
Return to your usual joy Oh my heart
To once more experience those beauties of love
If only she could but let it be.

From the bottom of my lonely heart
I have often cried for you
That you might incline your ears to me.
I still wait for you to hear my pleas
To satisfy and show my innermost feelings for you
And my woes will forever flee from me
For I will love you through the times to come.

Open those latched floodgates of my heart
That abundant love for you might flow with ease
For in grief and in chains it lies afraid.
Alak and alas, I cry for you to come to me
My heart I have poured out to you Oh my love
That we might find a common ground,
For though caged, our love seems to flow with ease.
Though heads or tails it's all the same to us,
Let's fulfill and share the love we have—
Love, that thief that has stolen my heart.
Oh how I love you my lovely love
Oh my love, how I love you!
Confusion and indecision have crept into me
From how I want you and want you the more.
My heart aches and a definite numbness grips my soul
For I love you and love as I have never loved before,
So come to me Oh my love
To cement this love with your lovely love.
Oh how I love you Oh my love!

This was how his mind worked. They were married, but that association had vanished from his thoughts. He now only saw her as that apple of his eyes. She was the one that he had approached as the wind, associated together with as the bottled wind and is about to loose again. She was about to be lost to another man. She was already lost to that other man as he saw it and it was time for him to lament his loss as he did the first time around.

He however suddenly came back to his senses. She was his wife, if not physically then at least mentally, but it was time to let go, if he could. He did love her so much, but it was time to let go.

Now that Johnny had collected firsthand information to the effect that Joy was not just unfaithful but also wanted to set him up for a divorce, he was ready to act. It was now obvious to him that a leopard can never change its spots. One can never tame a wolf and expect that it will never behave like a wild animal again.

Joy was into the escort business and her actions now points to the fact that she was not too far from that now. The state of matrimony might have tempered her down a little bit, but it was not able to erase it off from her altogether. He was going to make the first move towards getting unhitched, that way her plans would come to nothing. He would have never imagined that she could make such a plan.

It was very heart breaking for him to watch his wife being made love to by another man. It was even more heart breaking to find out that the man involved was one of his junior workers. To add salt to injury, this was the very man that he had hired despite being aware of his shortcomings. He fumed with anger and rage at first, but reality soon dawned on him. He was at fault. He hired him and he married her despite knowing what each of them was. She had even tried to warn him right at the beginning but he was not ready to listen.

The best option would be for him to let it go, and that was actually the only viable option. He was going to be diplomatic about it. He let them leave first before making it back home.

He was welcomed back home with jubilation. Joy pretended that she had been missing him for too long. He respected her, at least for being a very good actress. He knew that she was just acting, but she did not know that he knew that. He even began to suspect that she had been acting all along.

As soon as they got into the room she pounced on him. She must be a nymphomaniac, and that was all that went through his mind. He decided to play along with her, but he had one funny plan. He was going to give her one heck of a love performance—the type that she would never forget. The idea was to give her something that she would miss for the rest of her life. He had watched her with Tommy Boy and he knew that when it came to technics and the ability to satisfy her, they were not in the same league at all. She was probably only trying to play him too. He felt sorry for him; Tommy Boy that is.

As soon as she let go, he dropped his brief case to the floor and began to unbutton his shirt. He tried to help her unbutton hers too. He knew what she wanted and he was going to deliver. His shirt was off in no time while his pant and underwear dropped to the floor miraculously. To show how much he had missed her, he literarily ripped off her half unbuttoned blouse. She loved it. It showed the animal in him and that was a testimony to his virility.

He wheeled her round and embraced her from the back, she knew his plan. He began to squeeze her breasts with a combination of rubbing and stroking especially around her nipples. He felt them stiffen and then harden while growing a little bit larger. A lot of goose bumps suddenly erupted all around them. He knew that she was already aroused. This was confirmed with fast shallow breaths as well as a couple of faint deep guttural grunts.

He then let his right hand reluctantly slide down to somewhere between her legs. At first he caressed the inner parts of her thighs while still playing with her breasts. She then began to shiver and moan while at the same time taking up one of her legs to the edge of the bed. The idea was to give him an easier access to her now raging womanhood. He then let his fingers go further up into the cleft.

As soon as his ring finger hit her clitoris, she jerked backwards as if she did not want that. She however immediately reversed that move in order to fully present it to that finger. At first he rubbed it and she moaned the more. It was at this stage that he wheeled her round to face him. It was only to discover that her facial expression only indicated that she was gone. She did not know where she was and this was due to overexcitement. He then knelt down for cunilingus.

With his lips now locked in to cover her entire vaginal area, he began to employ his tongue. He let it tease and play around that vestigial protuberance. That was more than enough to trigger off a series of short jerks as well as ohohs. She held tight to his head and made every effort to get that tongue further in, or at least make sure that it never stopped what it was doing.

Her tiny erection was now as much erect as it could get. He would now take a little nip at it once in a while and that made her always shout for joy. It was a totally new experience and she was already being knocked senseless by it. He licked all around, but he knew when to ease off a little bit. That made her hover around the edge of orgasm for a long time while sweating it out. She was now completely immersed in that abyss of sexual passion and there was no going back. She wanted it and she wanted it badly. All her muscles had stiffened beyond belief and he knew what was about to happen. He always brought her to the edge before letting off.

This was the first time that he realized that Joy was a very strong lady. She grabbed his head and her hands felt like a vise. She made every possible attempt to push his face further against her gaping hole. On his part, he was making as much effort as possible to avoid suffocation. It was at that moment that she began to jerk uncontrollably and wildly. He had triggered off a series of orgasms in her, the magnitude of which no one could ever vouch to. It lasted quite a while without being attended to.

While this was still going on, he stood up and in one fluid movement scooped her up. He then laid her on the floor. She suspected what he was about to do and it was a very welcome idea. He went down to continue from where he stopped, but it was getting too much for her. She tried to push him away while asking him to stop. That was one of those equivocal and inexplicable situations when it came to feminine sexuality. She wanted him to stop, but in reality she wanted him the more—more than she had ever wanted that thing that was happening to her.

He had continued on the floor with his tongue. His mouth was now too wet with some fluid and so he changed to using his fingers. It was a very methodical approach. One finger was on her clitoris, two stroked all over her labia on either side while the thumb took care of the area just above the clitoris. The last finger was inside! This last one searched and searched. One could never tell what it was searching for, but eventually it hit her G—spot. Please don't ask me what this spot is because I don't know. All I know is that it made her go bananas with excitement. It could have been one particular spot or maybe several spots. It was a combination of supersensitive spots and then he hit all of them together.

The result of the combined effect of those five fingers was to send her off to wherever it was that she went to. Most probably to paradise on earth. She gave a series of stringed up erratic moans as well as moans mixed with loud sighs. Her face was contorted as if she was in pain. If it was pain, then it was the very pleasurable type of pain for she demanded some more of it. All her muscles had become as stiff as rock and she now looked like a classic body builder.

It is claimed that "he that is down fears no fall." Here is the proof that it is a wrong statement. She was on the floor but she groped at anything within arm's reach as if to prevent herself from falling. One hand grabbed the foot of the bed and held tight while the other took hold of the sofa. For each of those hands, it was a vice-like grip. Initially her lower region thrust upwards and downwards with deliberately slow but screwing motion. This increased in strength and frequency till it got to a wild uncontrollable stage. It was at this stage that she began to swing her head from side to side with total pleasure. She also kept muttering in unknown tongues. He could not understand what incoherencies came out of her mouth. She did not even know what she was saying either.

At first he thought that they were French words but that was just because French was claimed to be the language of love. At one time he thought that they were either Spanish or Portuguese words, but he was a complete dunce when it came to other languages. He only knew about English. His imagination had led him to believe that those words were a compound language that came from a mixture of Hebrew, that dead language Latin, and Igbo, all infused with some clicking language signs from the Hotentort pigmy tongue. It was at this juncture that her entire body began to vibrate wildly. The vibration increased in intensity till it reached an apparent crescendo that marked the height of that particular series of orgasms before it began to ebb.

It was at this stage that he let his fingers rest, but he inserted his manhood! Good gracious! The experience was indescribable. He did and could not reconsider before inserting it with ell ferociousness, paying complete disregard to caution for he was already too high to care. She on her part was now fully wet and her inside full of juice. He thrust up and down in total disregard and she responded in like manner as well as in complete unison, while now grabbing him tightly with both hands and legs.

He let the thrusts come from either side, from both top and bottom as well as straight from the center. He let them come at random and she enjoyed it as she had never done before. Once in a while she would tear at him while shouting: 'please more!'. Of course there was nothing more that he could offer. He had done the most that he could. He was inconsiderate and he was non-sympathetic as he pounded away though at the same time compassionate. How those three words came to be together there, even he himself was not sure of that. The important thing is that he strived to give it all to her.

She suddenly began to speak once more in those forgotten tongues. However, this time around they came as uncompleted clauses and phrases in-between gasps and they were essentially incomprehensible to either of them. She had been raised to such a height of passion and pleasure that she had virtually lost her power of coherent speech.

She was at the height of her arousal and desire. Extreme ecstasy had transported her to heights way beyond that enchanted zone of paradise. One piercing cry of joy followed another as he let both palms take hold of her derriere in an attempt to thrust them further up and go deeper into her.

The fire had been fanned to produce more flames. The fire of passion had been lifted to a still higher level—a level that one could not have been able to even contemplate. She then began to attempt to grab at anything that came her way and yet was not able to hold on to any of them. That was when the inner walls of her vagina began to contract on their own accord. They did so in such a way that they tended to draw him further in into her. That was too much for him and his own muscles suddenly began to contract. She wanted it all, and she wanted it all far and deep inside her.

It was the premonition that something big was about to happen that once more came to him. It was such that he could no longer control his own actions. He had gone deaf and could no longer hear her moans neither was he able to hear those words that came from her mouth any more. His urethral as well as other sphincters around that zone began to contract and relax and his own fluid began to jet into her in spurts. They came with such force and speed that he was sure they were able to find their ways as far up as into her stomach. She felt the same way too and later confessed that she even thought that some had jetted their way up to very near her throat.

It was like bliss. It was bliss. She came once more at that very moment and they both felt that final pleasure together. It was the most joyful and most satisfying as well as energy sapping coitus they had ever had. They collapsed into each other's arms completely winded, exhausted as well as light headed and empty and yet totally fulfilled. They were each completely worn out and out of breath and they needed a well-deserved rest.

They were each still panting in very shallow breaths when Johnny began to speak:

"Joy."

"Yes darling."

"Did you miss me?"

"Completely."

"I don't think I could ever do this with another person."

"Do what?" She asked while beginning to get a little bit suspicious that he meant something that is not as simple as he sounded.

"Make love."

"Me too."

"Are you sure?"

"I can swear to that." She replied a little bit afraid as to what he could have found out. There was a short pause for effect before he continued:

"Are you sure that you cannot make out with another man even if I recommend it?"

"How dare you think of that?"

"But in some cultures, a lady is allowed to have more than one husband at a time."

"Like where for instance?"

"I've forgotten the name of the place, but it is an ancient culture. In fact it was rumored that in that very same culture a man had a queer way of showing how much of a friend his friend was. He could be so friendly with another man that he would not mind sharing his most cherished association with him."

"I don't quite get that."

"If his friend visits him, instead of offering him some drinks, he could ask him to go to bed with his wife while he waits in the sitting room for them to finish."

"Are you planning to offer me to another person?"

"Who knows?"

"God forbid! Till you remember the name of the place let's close that topic."

"That means that you are afraid to discuss that."

"Not afraid. Just that it is an outrageous suggestion."

"In what way is it outrageous?"

"It is also meaningless."

"Even if the friend does so without the husband's permission?"

"Are you sure that you are mentally all right?"

"Are you sure that you are not avoiding the topic out of guilty conscience?"

That was enough to make her go back into her actress's role. She looked and sounded as if she was totally angry and shouted at him:

"What are you insinuating?"

"That walls have ears and I believe that you had cheated on me."

"What do you mean by that?"

"That you must have broken your marital vows behind me."

"It's a pity you think that way. For your information I am not like most of those other women who go about doing so."

"Who do you know that does that?"

"At least sixty percent of the women I know do that, and even more in the case of men."

"In other words you want to join the majority."

"We have never had this type of discussion before. Where did it come from?"

"From rumors that had filtered through the walls."

"Like which rumors?"

"The one that you have been making out with Tommy Boy."

He was watching her very closely as he mentioned that name. She was a very good actress, but that was too much for her. Her face immediately blanched out. There was also that look on it that tended to suggest that she had just been caught in the act.

"Johnny love; from where did you hear such preposterous rumor?"

"From Tommy boy's fiancée."

"Tommy Boy's fiancée?"

"Yes. Don't you know her?"

"No. I did not know that he was engaged."

"Now you know. She was not happy that you were messing around with her man and for that reason she came to blow the whistle on you." There was a short pause before he added: "So what is going on between the two of you?"

"Nothing. Nothing at all; and please don't ask such crazy questions again."

"You should have rather asked how I found out."

"Found out what?"

"That you and Tommy boy have been having quality time together."

"Not on my life. A jealous woman is capable of all sorts of imaginations and stories. Please try and disregard whatever stories she had told you."

"What of when you both travelled out for recruitment?"

"What about then?"

"Why did you have to share the same room with him?"

"I did not."

"Do you remember the lady who always served you in the room?"

"What do you mean? Are you now clairvoyant too?"

"At times."

"And what about her?"

"She happened to be a sister to one of the two women that you travelled with. She told her everything."

"I am a respectable married woman Johnny. Even if I stayed in the same room with that weasel nothing will happen. Trust me."

"I trust you. After all when I met you, you were with a married bishop."

"That was history."

"Is he now a weasel?"

"What else could he be?"

"Your sweet heart I guess."

"Stop that Johnny."

Johnny had been watching her. He now knew that this woman was one tough cookie. She was not going to crack that easy. He had to shift gears. If she did so without his knowing he would not mind; and even if he found out all she had to do was to apologize and it would be over. She simply kept denying. He therefore had to change tactics.

"Where were you when I just travelled?"

"Right here missing you."

"Were you ever at Hotel Excelsior?"

"No."

"Not even with Tommy Boy there?"

She was now obviously worried and she seemed to be in deep thought for about two minutes. He let her have as much time as she wanted without interruption. Then her facial expression changed. It was like 'eureka!' She had just remembered.

"Aha. Now I remember. Four of us went there the other day for a business lunch."

"Okay Joy, let me stop beating about the bush. This is a very small town and everyone here knows each other, especially when it comes to me. It is for this reason that they all know you too. You made the mistake of frequenting there with Tommy Boy and they told me all about it."

"Just for that innocent Lunch?"

"No."

"No to what?"

"You went all the way each time you were there."

"Who floated that type of rumor over to you?"

"I can see that none of you knows who the manager of that hotel is. He used to be my private driver and I secured that job for him. He told me everything that went on there."

"Don't mind him."

"Joy. I was there too."

"What do you mean?"

"I did not travel at all. You and Tommy boy were using room six hundred and two. I was in room six hundred and four just next to you."

"Okay we were there together, but I never yielded. I did not want people to see us in the dining room together and so we opted to dine in one of the rooms."

"I hope you still remember that saying that walls have ears?"

"Yes."

"I heard and saw everything that went on in that room for the entire three days that I was supposed to have travelled."

This was enough to finally make her turn completely white and look very afraid and concerned as well as confused for the first time. Johnny however continued:

"The room was bugged, and I both heard and watched everything that went on in that room for three days. I had several copies of the tape of your activities there."

She went down on her knees before him and started to beg for mercy and forgiveness. She asked him to remember how God forgave those who sinned, even David when he did things that were worse than that. He was not moved; instead he had his own counter argument. According to him, it was God that forgave and so he was not going to offend Him by taking that prerogative away from him. God forgives, and he was not going to do so.

"Do you know how much pain you have caused me? Do you know how excruciatingly painful it could be for a man to watch another man make love to his wife? Of course you will never understand. I will never forgive you! I heard you tell him of your plans for me. You told him how you had set me up, especially in regard to Halima, and how you planned to get half of all my worth. Well that would not be possible now.

"I have already given a copy of the tape to the police and another to my lawyer. If you do not want any embarrassments, you might be better off packing your things and checking out of the house. We can always arrange for the annulment of the marriage later."

Johnny had been hurt, and he hurt really bad. He was as green with envy as envy itself as he watched another man on his wife. He did not however bear any grudges against any of them. Right now all he wanted was to extricate himself free of her. She used to be a source of pleasure and bliss, but now she had changed to an object of discomfort.

She had done this with total disregard to the effect it was going to have on her partner. It was her reluctance and eventual refusal to part with her past that had led to this situation. She had succeeded in managing to break up the marriage. From now on they were going to live apart from each other, and as for Johnny, his aim was to set her free.

Now that she had been disentangled or unhitched as she would put it, from those drudgeries and restrictions of conjugal existence, she would be free to follow her heart once more. She obviously lacked even the merest iota of moral codes and ethical principles. She was a free spirited individual who needed to be set free. It was her beauty and apparent external decorum that tended to hide those her pit falls. It was obvious that regular impropriety was an ingrained part of her character. Once more, a leopard can never change his spots at will. Incidentally she did not believe that he had any tapes at all.

Joy had packed her things and was on her way out of the house before changing her mind. She had been caught red-handed, but there was nothing wrong with giving her own plan a try. One can never tell what was going to be the outcome. Even if it did not work, that would be no problem, after all it is claimed that he that is down needs fear no fall. If Johnny puts her out then she would be down. If her plan failed then she would still be down. There was however that possibility that she was going to be successful, no matter how remote that possibility might be.

She unpacked her things and then decided to turn nasty. She promptly informed Johnny that if anyone had to leave the house he was the one that had to leave. They were married and that made them one. To split therefore they had to split their properties too for everything that he owned belonged to them both. They had been united in holy matrimony. Furthermore, she pointed out to him, he was the person who brought her out of her house to his own and so the onus was on him to provide for her even if they were to split up. If he did not do that, then he was going to make her homeless as it were.

She ended up by pointing it out to him that they just had to share the house and that was that. Johnny did not like that idea, but he did not seem to have much choice in the matter. He did not see how they could live there together as a separated couple. He was not too sure of what she had in mind but one thing was clear, she had a very devilish mind. She must have a plan of her own, but he was sure that he was equal to it. All he had to do was to wait and see.

It was not long before Johnny found out what her plan was. He was at work the following morning when a hand-delivered letter came from her lawyer. She was suing him for divorce on the grounds of adultery and irreconcilable differences. Johnny was taken aback when that letter arrived. It meant that she was rather too fast for him and things were going to get nasty.

Johnny had to take his own steps. He summoned the company's lawyer, who incidentally was his roommate at college. He told the lawyer what had happened before showing him the letter. He perused the letter and thought for a while before offering his own suggestion.

He advised Johnny to contact Jim Barry who was their classmate in school. He was now a celebrated divorce attorney, though he lived in another state. There was really nothing to it. He was sure that with Jimmy handling the case, he would have things his own way. He was advised not to give it a second thought. In their state, the law had that tendency to favor the wife in divorce cases, but in this particular case it might be different. She was definitely at fault and so not the person to file the case. As for infidelity, even if proved, it was no longer grounds for divorce anymore. This is because infidelity had come to be more common than faithfulness. It had come to be the norm rather than the exception. In fact some comedians had recommended that couples should be divorced whether they like it or not, for being too faithful to each other, or for not violating their marital vows.

Johnny made a couple of calls and that evening Jimmy flew into town. He happened to be the private lawyer to the president of the country. For this reason alone, he had all sorts of contacts in high places both politically and within the judicial circles.

For that evening, both Jimmy and he stayed together in a hotel in town. It was while they were there that he played that tape for him. Jimmy consoled him for what had happened. According to him, he could feel the pain in his heart, and he knew the pain was going to be worse now that he was the accused.

Johnny had been accused of philandering with his secretary Halima. She gave specific instances and the most specific was during that his international trip with her. In court Johnny gave a full account of his travels and presented documents to support whatever he said. He was found clean at the end of his interrogation. Jimmy had promised him that the case was very straight forward. It was going to be a slam dunk and he therefore never gave it any more thought.

Johnny had never felt more relaxed as the case went on. He actually gained a couple of pounds in weight within a few days as it went on. He was the one that felt that if she ever left him he was going to commit suicide. As it were, she had helped him get over it with this case. This false accusation had helped him out a lot. Rather than worry about her loss as he would have expected, he was now out to get even. Unfaithfulness was nothing new in town, what was new was her action.

He had lost quite a bit of weight when he was still thinking of how he was going to lose her to another man. Now he was gaining weight as he thought of how to extract vengeance from her. His only mistake, as he now found out, was to have married her. His eyes had done the thinking for him rather than his brains. He had opted for beauty and decorum rather than character and he had gotten hitched to her rather than getting married to her. To her, she was just tagging along for the lucre and that helped him understand why she had insisted on its having been getting hitched. He did not blame her because she had warned him right at the beginning, but he was not ready to listen. It was all his fault. He did not however blame himself either because it was then that he realized the full meaning of the saying that 'love is blind.'

The case had started within three weeks from when those summons were served. Jimmy had however transferred the case to a different court. He had insisted that the first court was situated within an old building and he was allergic to certain things there. Phobia was the term that he added. His wishes were granted and the case was transferred to the court of Judge Martello. There was however a totally different reason for him to do that.

It is claimed that judges are completely impartial when delivering judgment, irrespective of personal experiences. That had come to be a purely theoretical supposition. The experience through which this particular judge had gone through had always remained a secret. Jimmy however knew about it and he was going to exploit it to the fullest. Long before he became a senior judge, he had gone through exactly the same experience as Johnny. He had caught his wife in bed with another man. To make matters worse, he was an ex-prisoner; and to add further salt to injury, he was the person who had helped put the man away. The difference was that it took place in his own bed. He did not mind her going astray once in a while, what he hated was its happening right on his own bed.

His wife was a medical doctor that treated prisoners and it was during her encounters with the prisoners that they met, she and the ex-convict that is. She had arranged for his escape from prison. Most embarrassingly however was the fact that there was a three month man hunt without his being found. All this time the man was hiding in his house and having a nice time with his own wife. He was a very handsome inmate then, and when the doc. asked why he was always around when it did not seem that much was wrong with him, he explained it away as that he had that crush on her. Her problem is that she always had a soft spot for those whose freedoms and liberties were being curtailed. One thing led to another, as it is often put, and they eventually fell for each other.

Their nemesis was that the judge had forgotten one of his files at home and so had returned barely half an hour after leaving home. It was only to find his wife naked with the fugitive right in his own bed. Lo and behold, it was that escaped criminal making it out with his wife in his house. He was furious that they did not go to a hotel for that. He did not mind her going out with others, after all, as he often put it, it can never get exhausted, it had no meter and it will still remain there, so why should he worry. He quickly called in the police and the man was rearrested.

During his retrial, the criminal's lawyer argued that it was the doctor who put the idea of getting involved with each other into the head of his client. Beyond that he also argued that she was the person who spirited him out of the prison simply for personal reasons. She had turned him into a sex slave, raped him more than several times and indeed held him against his will. He was able to prove all those accusations and she was found guilty. It was sweet music to his ears, her husband that is. She was found guilty on all counts and sentenced for them. Her lover was returned to jail with a few more years added for the escape. The judge did not buy into the kidnapping story though.

While waiting for sentencing, she filed for divorce. She told the court that it was his sexual deviations and abuse at home that led her into what she did. The judge had however insisted that those accusations lacked even the slightest merit. She was sentenced to ten years in prison with hard labor. The divorce was granted and the husband was asked to determine the conditions.

With that very bitter experience at the back of his mind, the judge was likely going to have a soft spot for Johnny. It was not going to be because Joy was unfaithful, for that was nothing new or rare, but because she had tried to blackmail him. Many will temper justice with mercy, he was likely going to temper and deliver it with experience. It was the type of experience that was going to be with one for his entire life.

When the case started most people were sure that Joy was going to win. This was not because they were on her side, but it was because of how it was presented. Moreover none of them knew of those tapes. Her lawyer was a very smart and costly one, but he was about to experience a new type of judgment.

According to Joy, Johnny had always been very unfaithful to her and was deeply steeped into extramarital affairs. He always broke his marital vows with impunity. She claimed that it was common knowledge that he provided freely for his secretary Halima. She claimed that he took her along for the trips just as an escort. She explained that they jetted around the world at will, not for business trips as it was claimed, but for amorous trysts. Her lawyer had intimated that the only reason that he always travelled with her was to keep their sexual encounters as secret as possible. Most of the unlookers tended to see it that way too.

To drive home their points, they brought in a few witnesses. They were workers from the company and each pointed out that they had always heard those rumors. According to her lawyer, these witnesses were men and women of impeccable characters and their contributions should be taken seriously. Jimmy on his part had pointed out that those were all rumors. He had cross examined each witness, and each of them had agreed that no one had ever witnesses them doing anything.

It was two full days of testimonies before it came to Johnny's turn. It was time for all to hear his own side of the story. His lawyer said that all he did with the prosecutors witnesses was to prove that what ever they said were based on rumors. He did not care to go further because whatever they said was completely irrelevant to the case. She had taken his last travel as a typical one. He had presented receipts as evidence that during their travels, they lived in separate hotels and each person ate in his or her own hotel. They were seen together only during the conferences and meetings where she took notes.

Finally came the bombshell! He told them that it was Joy who had been unfaithful during her recruitment tour and that Johnny knew about it, but he forgave her. She stayed and lived in the same room with Tommy Boy for those three days and there were ample evidences to prove that. He finally told the story of how Johnny had pretended to travel and yet he was in town. He finally requested that the other lawyer, the judge and he should meet in the judge's chamber. His request was granted.

Once within the chambers, he played the tape for them. The last travel was only a setup and Johnny was actually in town. He did not travel at all and when he told Joy about it she did not quite believe that the tape existed. He showed them the receipts to prove that Johnny was there, as well as his planes logbook to prove that the plane did not actually fly overseas during that period.

The judge knew firsthand how Johnny felt. He had experienced the same and he did not want another man to experience the same. He was completely on Johnny's side.

After the meeting, Joy's lawyer took her out for a short discussion before they both came back in. He asked that he and his client should be allowed to approach the bench. His request was granted. They were there for less than a minute before going back to their table. The judge then announced that there were new developments in the case. All allegations against Johnny had been withdrawn. Joy was to pay all legal expenses; both to her lawyer, Johnny's lawyer as well as all the court fees.

As for his ruling, He granted her the divorce that she has sued for. However he pointed out that she was rich enough to part without gaining anything from the marriage. He was of the opinion that she had gone into the marriage with the sole aim of getting divorced eventually and making off with a lot of money. If however Johnny decides to give anything to her, it was all left to him. It was not understandable and not easily comprehensible for one to see why the guilty in a particular case could sue the innocent. According to the judge, she was a patented gold digger.

There was a lot of tongue wagging going on after the case. It did not however take too long for them to find out the truth of the matter. Both Joy and Tommy Boy had to quit their jobs based on advice from the company. They were to quit peacefully or be fired. According to the grape vine, they had quit and each had gone his or her separate way.

That was how Johnny had successfully chased the wind; successfully bottled the wind and had finally successfully managed to unbottle that very same wind, for the wind can never be held captive.